OWEN BOOTH is a journalis[...] [...]
two sons. He lives in Walthams[...] [...]
2015 *White Review* Short Story Prize and was recently awarded 3rd prize in the Moth Short Story competition. His work has been published in numerous print and online magazines and anthologies.

Praise for *What We're Teaching Our Sons*:

'If you like the structure – set-up, joke, set-up, joke, set-up, joke – then you'll love *What We're Teaching Our Sons*. The book is not just funny: there are tiny stories embedded throughout the endlessly repeated pattern, as if a Bridget Riley painting were populated between the lines with lots of Bruegel micro-portraits'   IAN SANSOM, *Guardian*

'Booth pulls the rug out from under the novel form – not to mention a card-house of masculine archetypes – with tender, satirical, melancholy ease'

JOANNA WALSH, author of *Break.up*

'Formally bold, funny, sweetly sad and fiendishly clever, Booth finds, on the journey men take with their boys, a small, fertile, hitherto undiscovered island somewhere in the vast ocean between Donald Barthelme and Nick Hornby'

WILL ASHON, author of *Strange Labyrinth*

'As this comic tour de force testifies, Booth is a miniaturist. His meticulous craft bears more than a passing resemblance to that of his hobbyists, all those haunted men who seem to pour an excess of emotion into elaborate displacement activities. The novel's repetitive format and collective narrative voice provide a safety net of impersonality, allowing the tenderest of moments to bloom in the nooks and crannies of its vignettes' ANDREW GALLIX, *Literary Review*

'*What We're Teaching Our Sons* is remarkable. Booth has shone a light on the beautiful, flawed and complicated relationship between fathers and sons. I imagine there will be several bought, lent and lost copies of this book in my future'

LAURA PEARSON, *Motherload*

'This is a warm, funny, touching collection of thoughts on what it means in today's world to be a man … perfect for a tired new dad' ELAINE ROBB, *The Pool*

'Frighteningly well-observed, caustically perceptive, but never cynical … one of the pleasures, beyond the wit and exuberance of the prose, is the joy of seeing a writer finding the absolutely perfect form for their work'

LUKE KENNARD, author of *The Transition*

What We're Teaching Our Sons

Owen Booth

4th ESTATE • London

4th Estate
An imprint of HarperCollins*Publishers*
1 London Bridge Street
London SE1 9GF

www.4thEstate.co.uk

First published in Great Britain in 2018 by 4th Estate
This 4th Estate paperback edition published in 2019

1

A catalogue record for this book is
available from the British Library

ISBN 978-0-00-828262-2

Printed and bound in Great Britain by
CPI Group (UK) Ltd, Croydon, CRO 4YY

MIX
Paper from
responsible sources
FSC™ C007454

To Stan and Arthur

The Great Outdoors

We're teaching our sons about the great outdoors.

We're teaching them how to appreciate the natural world, how to understand it, how to survive in it. As concerned fathers have apparently been teaching their sons since the Palaeolithic.

We're teaching our sons how to make fires and lean-to shelters, how to tie twenty-five different kinds of knot, how to construct animal traps from branches and vines. We're teaching them how to catch things, how to kill things, how to gut things. Out on the frozen marshes before dawn we produce hundreds of rabbits out of sacks, try to show our sons how to skin the rabbits.

Our sons look over our shoulders, distracted by the beautiful sunrise. They don't want anything to do with skinning rabbits.

Out on the frozen marsh we explain the importance of being self-sufficient, and capable, and knowing the names of different cloud formations and geological features, and how to identify birds by their song.

'Cumulonimbus,' we say. 'Cirrus. Altostratus. Terminal moraine. Blackbird. Thrush. Wagtail.'

We hand out fact sheets and pencils, collect the rabbits. We promise prizes to whoever can identify the most types of trees.

'Can we set things on fire again?' our sons ask.

The stiff grass creaks under our feet as we make our way back to the car park. The sky is the colour of rusted copper.

'Can we set fire to a car?'

'No, you can't set fire to a car,' we say. 'Why would you want to set fire to a car?'

'To see what would happen,' our sons mutter, sticking their bottom lips out.

We look at our sons, half in fear, wondering what we have made.

Drowning

We're teaching our sons about drowning.

We tell them how we almost drowned when we were four years old. How we can still remember the feeling of being dragged along the bottom of the swollen river, the gravel in our faces, the smell of the hospital that lingered for weeks afterwards.

We don't want this to happen to our sons. Or worse.

We take our sons swimming every Sunday morning, try to teach them how to stay afloat. Each week we have to find a new swimming pool, slightly further from where we live, slightly more overcrowded. The council is methodically demolishing all the sports centres in the borough as part of the Olympic dividend.

We are being concentrated into smaller and smaller spaces.

In the water our sons cling to us. Our hundreds of sons. They splash and kick their legs gamely, but they don't seem to be getting any closer to being able to swim. We have to bribe them to put their faces under the water, and the price goes up every week.

We're sure it wasn't like this when we were children.

The water is a weird colour and tiles keep falling off the ceiling onto the swimmers' heads. A scum of discarded polystyrene cups floats in the corner of the pool. It's hotter than a sauna in here.

Also, we keep being distracted by the sight of the swim-suited mothers. The mothers who come in all sorts of fantastic shapes and sizes. They look as sleek as sea otters in their black swimsuits. They make us ashamed of our hairy backs, our formerly impressive chests, our pathetic tattoos.

We hope they can look at us with kinder eyes.

We crouch low in the water like middle-aged crocodiles, stealing glances at the sleek sea-otter mothers, and our sons put their arms around our necks and refuse to let go.

In the changing rooms we hold on to our sons' tiny, fragile bodies; feel the terrible responsibility of lost socks, and impending colds, and the effects of chlorine on skin and lungs. We wrap our sons in towels, blow dry their hair, try not to consider the future and all the upcoming catastrophes that we can't protect them from.

We promise ourselves that next week we'll get it right.

Heartbreak

We're teaching our sons about heartbreak.

Its inevitability. Its survivability. Its necessity. That sort of thing.

We take our sons to meet the heartbroken men. We have to show our credentials at the gate. We have a letter of introduction.

Our jeeps bounce across the rolling scrubland under huge blackening skies. As we approach the compound a group of men in camouflage gear watch us carefully. They all have beer bellies and assault rifles.

The heartbroken men are heartbroken on account of the breakdown of their marriages, and the fact that they never see their children, and the fact that they're earning less than they expected to be at this point in their lives, and the fact that no one takes them seriously any more. In their darkest moments the heartbroken men suspect that no one took them seriously before, either. The fathers of the heartbroken men loom large. Their hard-drinking, angry fathers. And their fathers and their fathers and their fathers before them.

The heartbroken men like to dress up as soldiers and superheroes. It's embarrassing. How are we supposed to respond?

We don't like the look of those skies.

'We have a manifesto,' the heartbroken men tell our sons. They want our sons to take their message back to the people. Their spokesmen step forward. There's a banner too. They're planning to hang it off a bridge or some other famous landmark.

'Are those real guns?' our sons ask.

'We –'

'Can we have a go on the guns?' our sons ask.

'No, you can't have a go on the guns,' we tell our sons. 'Don't let them have a go on the guns,' we tell the heartbroken men, 'what were you even thinking?'

The heartbroken men go quiet. They look at their feet.

'Well?'

'Fathers are superheroes,' the heartbroken men say, quietly.

'What?'

'Superheroes,' say the heartbroken men, starting to cry. Tears roll down their cheeks and fall upon the barren, scrubby ground.

This is turning into a disaster.

We should never have come.

Philosophy

We're teaching our sons about philosophy.

We're discussing logic, metaphysics, ethics and aesthetics. We're covering philosophical methods of inquiry, the philosophy of language, the philosophy of mind. We're asking our sons to consider 'if there is something that it is like to be a particular thing'.

We're on a boat trip up a Norwegian fjord and our sons are gathered on deck to listen to our lecture series. The spectacular mountains slide by as we talk about the sublime. The steel deck is wet from the recent rain.

Our sons are doing their best to feign interest, we have to give them that. They're disappointed that there are no whales or polar bears to look at.

We're trying to remember which famous philosopher lived in a hut up a Norwegian fjord.

Not all the children on deck are our sons. The boat is full

of beautiful, strapping Norwegian teens on a school trip. They're all six foot tall with no sense of personal space. They make our sons look stunted and reserved. They keep asking our sons if they have any crisps. This has been going on for five days and everyone is getting sick of it.

'Why are we here?' our sons ask us.

'Yes!' we say, pointing to our sons with the chalk, like we've seen lecturers do in films. 'That's exactly the crux of it!'

'No,' our sons say. 'Why are we here, on a boat, halfway up Norway? When we could be exactly just about anywhere else?'

We have no answer to that one.

In the evenings everyone eats together in the dining hall and then the older sons sneak off to try to get a glimpse of the beautiful Norwegian teen girls and boys who gather at the back of the boat singing folk songs and playing acoustic guitars. We put the younger sons to bed and tell them about Descartes and Spinoza, try to pretend we don't wish we were still teenagers.

Then we sit up long into the night nursing our glasses of aquavit and listening to the distant music and laughter.

We came to Norway in the hope of seeing the aurora borealis, but it's summer and the sun never sets.

Work

We're teaching our sons about work.

We're taking them to the office, the factory, the school, the hospital. They're coming with us on film shoots, on home visits, on our window-cleaning rounds. They're helping us to study the births and deaths of volcanic islands, to collect unpaid gambling debts, to project-manage billion-pound IT infrastructure transformation programmes.

Other children, we remind our sons, would be excited to see where their fathers work, what they do for a living.

We're teaching our sons that it's important to have a vocation. And that even if you don't have a vocation you still have to turn up every day and pretend you care. We're teaching our sons about compromise. We're teaching them how to skive, how to slack off, how to take credit for other people's work. We're teaching them how to negotiate pay rises and how to have office affairs.

We tell our sons the stories of our many office affairs, back in the good old, bad old days.

We tell them about our affair with beautiful Stephanie from reception, and the magnificent sunset in Paris, and the helicopter ride, and the horrible accident. We tell them about our affair with Cathy the kickboxing champion, and how it ended with a spectacular roundhouse kick to our head. The gay dads tell the stories of their affairs with Steve and Mark and Sunny and John and David and Disco Clive and the two Andrews. The mothers of our sons, overhearing, start to tell stories of their own wild workplace affairs, their own crazy and dangerous pasts, which makes us all a bit nervous.

We go on for a while, until our sons start to wander off.

They're convinced they're going to be film stars and astronauts and famous comic book artists. They're not interested in all the ways we managed to screw up our stupid lives.

Whales

We're teaching our sons about whales.

Their habits and habitats, their evolutionary history, their cultural and economic relevance, the many stories told about them.

An adult male sperm whale has washed up, dead, on a beach on the Norfolk coast, and we're following the clean-up effort on TV and the radio and the internet. People are worried that the build-up of gas inside the decomposing whale carcass may cause it to explode. Onlookers have been moved back to a safe distance.

Our sons are gripped by the unfolding drama.

We tell our sons about the long relationship between people and whales – about the whaling industry, and the historical uses of baleen and blubber and ambergris and whalebone. We tell them about the hunting of minke whales and pilot whales and bowhead whales and fin whales and sei whales and humpback whales and grey whales and so on. We tell them the stories of Jonah and the whale, and Moby Dick, and what we can remember of the plot of the film *Orca the Killer Whale*, and about the whale that got lost and swam up the Thames in 2006.

'Did you see the whale?' our sons ask, excitedly.

'Well no,' we say, 'we were out of the country at the time, but –'

'What happened to the whale?' our sons ask. 'Was it rescued?'

We explain to our sons that, despite the best efforts of various organisations to save it, the Thames whale died two days after it was first spotted, from convulsions caused by dehydration and kidney failure. Everyone was very sad, we say. People had taken to calling the whale 'Diana'. It was one of those moments when the whole nation comes together.

'Except you, because you were out of the country,' our sons say.

'Well that's true, yes,' we admit.

On the TV, scientists and whale removal experts and members of the local council are reviewing their options. Dynamite is considered. Or burial. Apparently the smell is becoming unbearable. Luckily it's winter, so the tourist trade hasn't been too adversely affected. Nobody knows what caused the whale to wash up here – whether it was illness or a wrong turn or just old age.

'Maybe he was murdered,' our sons say. 'Maybe sharks did it, or other whales. Maybe he had it coming. Maybe he was a *bad whale.*'

Eventually the experts decide to load the whale onto the back of an eighteen-wheel lorry. It takes two days to lay the temporary metal road across the beach, twelve hours to roll the corpse of the whale onto a cradle, hoist it up onto the trailer, tie it down under yards of tarpaulin and plastic sheeting.

Then, under cover of night, a police escort leads the lorry and its stinking cargo through the dark lanes of East Anglia.

At an undisclosed location, the television reports tell us, tissue samples will be taken and the whale will be cut up and incinerated.

And we will be left to explain to our sons what the whole thing means.

Grandfathers

We're teaching our sons about their grandfathers.

Their silent, phlegmatic grandfathers who have survived wars and fifty-year marriages. Their grandfathers who are spending their retirement building model worlds out of balsa wood, plastic and flock.

We go round to see the grandfathers. We give the secret password. The loft hatch opens and a ladder is lowered. We usher our sons up the ladder, up into the darkness.

The grandfathers have been working up here for the last five years, tunnelling further back into the eaves, back into their own pasts.

At first they managed to maintain their relationships with their wives by coming down for meals and at bedtimes. They still mowed the lawn at weekends. Interacted with neighbours. Read the paper in the evening.

Then they built a system of pulleys that meant they could

have their food sent up to them, so they could eat while they worked. The lawn grew wild. Social occasions were missed. Eighteen months ago they started sleeping among the miles of miniature railway track, the half-finished buildings, the replica suspension bridges and goods yards. Waking up to find the trains had been running all night, the endless tiny whirr and clatter rattling through their dreams.

The grandmothers, with their own interesting lives to lead, barely notice their husbands' absence any more.

Fairy lights run the length of the roof, hanging above the miniature town like stars. Below, a single evening in the lives of the grandfathers is perfectly recreated in OO scale. The trolley buses. Posters outside the old cinema. People leaving work. A dark swell on the surface of the water in the harbour.

The families of the grandfathers, everything they own packed in suitcases, waiting at the station.

And the grandfathers themselves, as boys, searching desperately through the streets for their own silent, unknowable fathers.

We tell our sons not to touch anything, even as they grab for a small model dog and accidentally sideswipe an entire bus queue with their sleeve. The youngest knocks over a crane and causes a minor disaster down at the docks. The older boys attempt to engineer horrific train crashes.

The grandfathers set about them, us, with their belts. Chase us, yelling, from the loft.

'We forgive you!' we scream, as the grandfathers pursue us down the street.

Women

We're teaching our sons about women.

What they mean. Where they come from. Where they're headed, as individuals and as a gender.

We remind our sons that their mothers are women, that their cousins are women, that their aunts are women, that their grandmothers are women. The mothers of our sons confirm their status. They're intrigued to know where we're going with this.

We take our sons to art galleries and museums where they can look at women as they have been depicted for hundreds of years.

In the art galleries the security guards eye us warily, watch to make sure our sons don't go too near the valuable paintings and sculptures. There is a security guard in every room, sitting in a chair, keeping an eye on the art. The security guards are all different ages and sizes and shapes. At least half of them are women. There are arty young women and middle-aged women with glasses and older women with severe, asymmetrical haircuts.

Our sons stand in front of the works of art, under the watchful eyes of the security guards. In the works of art young women in various states of undress alternately have mostly unwanted sexual experiences or recline on and/or against things. They recline on and/or against sofas and mantelpieces and beds and picnic blankets and tombs and marble steps and piles of furs and ornamental pillars and horses and cattle. Some of the women are giant-sized. They sprawl across entire rooms in the museum. Their naked breasts and hips loom over our sons like thunder clouds.

'Is that what all women look like with no clothes on?' our sons ask us, nervously.

'Some of them,' we say, nodding, relying on our extensive experience. 'Not all.'

Our sons gaze up at the giant women, awed. They sneak glances at the women security guards, try to make sense of it all.

'What do women want?' our sons ask.

We notice the women security guards looking at us with interest. We consider our words carefully.

'Maybe the same as the rest of us?' we say.

The women security guards are still staring at us.

'Somewhere to live,' we add. 'A sense of purpose. Food. Dignity, most likely.'

'What about adventure?' our sons ask. 'What about fast cars? What about romance?'

We look over at the women security guards, hoping for a sign.

We're not getting out of this one that easily.

Money

We're teaching our sons about money.

We're teaching them that money is the most important thing there is. We're teaching them that they can never have enough money, that their enemies can never have too little. We're teaching them that money has an intrinsic worth beyond the things that it can buy, that money is a measure of their worth as *men*.

Alternatively, we're teaching our sons that money is an illusion. That it doesn't matter at all. That, most of the time, it doesn't even exist.

'Look at the financial industry,' we tell them. 'Look at derivatives. Look at credit default swaps. Look at infinite rehypothecation.'

Our sons nod at us, blankly. They're not old enough for any of this. What were we thinking?

Together with our sons we go on the run, hiding out in a

series of anonymous motels. The receptionists accept our false names without asking any questions. At three in the morning we peer out through the blinds or the heavy curtains, look for the lights of police cars out in the rain while our sons sleep.

'Who's out there?' our sons ask in their sleep. 'What do they want?'

We can't remember the last time we slept in our own beds, cooked a meal in our own kitchens. The mothers of our sons have indulged this nonsense for far too long.

Most importantly, we're teaching our sons how to make money. We're putting them to work as paper boys, as child actors, as tiny bodyguards. We're turning them into musical prodigies, poets and prize-winning authors. We're getting them to write memoirs of their troubled upbringings. We're using them to make false insurance claims. We're training them to throw themselves in front of cars and fake serious injuries.

And the cash is rolling in. We've had to buy a job lot of counting machines.

We sit up long into the night listening to the constant whirr of the counting machines as they sing the song of our growing fortune, and we watch the rise and fall of our beautiful sleeping sons' chests.

Geology

We're teaching our sons about geology.

We're teaching them about sedimentary, igneous and metamorphic rocks, about plate tectonics, about continental drift. We're teaching them about the history of the earth, and the fossil record, and deep time.

It's making us feel old.

Our sons want to learn about volcanoes, so we book an out-of-season holiday to Iceland. We stand on the edge of the Holuhraun lava field, staring down into the recently re-awoken inferno. Swarms of separate eruptions throw magma across the blackened, stinking landscape. Dressed in their silver heatproof suits, our sons look like an army of miniature henchmen.

We tell our sons about Eyjafjallajökull and Mount St Helens, about Krakatoa and Pompeii. We tell them how the eruption of Mount Tambora in 1815 led to a year without summer around the globe. We tell them about the supervolcano under Yellowstone park that may one day wipe out half the continental United States.

The spectacularly beautiful Icelandic tour guides – who are called Hanna Gunnarsdóttir and Solveig Gudrunsdóttir and Sigrun Eiðsdóttir – explain to our sons about Iceland's geothermal energy infrastructure, how a quarter of the country's electricity is generated using heat that comes directly from the centre of the earth.

Our sons try to get each other to run towards the lava flows, to see how close they can come before they burst into flames.

We are gently admonished by the spectacularly beautiful Icelandic tour guides for the behaviour of our sons. We are all a little bit in love with the spectacularly beautiful Icelandic tour guides. The mothers of our sons, of course, instantly become best friends with them and invite them to have a drink with us in the thermal pools.

In the thermal pools we drink incredibly expensive beers and watch the snow fall on our sons' shoulders, settle on their hair. Our sons shiver in the brittle air, splash and jump on each other. They remind us of Japanese snow monkeys.

Hanna Gunnarsdóttir and Solveig Gudrunsdóttir and Sigrun Eiðsdóttir explain to us about the geothermal systems that heat approximately eighty-five per cent of the country's buildings. They remind us that, geologically, Iceland is a young country: like our sons it is still being formed, as the mid-Atlantic ridge that splits the island right down the middle slowly pushes the North American and Eurasian tectonic plates away from each other.

We tell Hanna Gunnarsdóttir and Solveig Gudrunsdóttir and Sigrun Eiðsdóttir that we know how it must feel to be the western half of the country, helplessly watching the east speed towards the horizon at a rate of three centimetres a year. If only our sons were drifting away from us that slowly, we joke.

But they've already stopped listening.

Sport

We're teaching our sons about sport.

We're teaching them how to ride a bike, how to kick a ball, how to run at and go round and pick up and jump over stuff. We're giving them suggestions on how to choose a team to support.

Ideally we'd have outsourced a lot of this. It's not an area we have much expertise in. We don't tell our sons that.

'Throw the ball!' we shout at our sons, trying to get into the spirit of things. 'Catch it! Pass it! Hit it with the racquet/ bat/stick!'

Our sons stand in the middle of the sports field, looking at their hands like they don't know what they're for. Our beautiful, brilliant sons.

Our sons getting hit in the face. Our sons getting upended into the mud. Our sons getting trampled on. Our sons crashing their bikes into walls. Our sons falling off their skateboards. Our sons falling off trampolines and vaulting horses. Our sons missing catches, in slow motion. Our sons unable to climb ropes. Our sons with water up their noses, gasping for breath. Our sons slicing golf balls and swinging wildly at pitches and hooking penalties wide. Our sons tripping over their own feet. Our sons, gamely, getting back up again and again.

Our brave and magnificent sons.

We can't take it any more. We sprint onto the field, knocking small children flying in all directions, and scoop our beautiful sons up in our arms. Wipe the mud out of their eyes, the snot from their bashed-up noses.

And then, carrying our glorious, broken sons, we run.

Emotional Literacy

We're teaching our sons about emotional literacy.

We're teaching them about the importance of understanding and sharing their feelings, of not being stoic and trying to keep things bottled up.

Because we are aware of the concept of toxic masculinity, we're trying to make sure our sons grow into confident, well-balanced and emotionally open young men.

We've come to the park to ride on the miniature steam railway. The miniature steam railway is operated by a group of local enthusiasts who hate having to let children ride on their trains. The enthusiasts are all men.

'How are you feeling?' we shout to our sons, repeatedly, as we clatter around the track on the back of 1/8th scale trains. 'What's really going on with you? You can tell us. We're listening.'

Our sons pretend they haven't heard, try to ignore us. We

don't blame them. We can't imagine talking about our feelings with other men either. The idea is horrifying. That's why we all have hobbies.

We explain to our sons about our hobbies. About constructing and collecting and quantifying things, about putting stuff in order. Classic albums. Sightings of migratory birds. Handmade Italian bicycles. Like our fathers and their fathers and their fathers before them.

All those unknowable, infinitely quantifiable fathers.

Two of the steam enthusiasts are arguing with a customer who keeps letting his children stand up while the train is moving. Nobody wants to give ground. Eventually the customer leaves the park with his kids. He's coming back, though, he tells us all. He's going to sort this out.

We imagine the stand-off between the gang of ageing steam enthusiasts and the angry posse that the dissatisfied customer has, we assume, gone to recruit. The fist-fights on top of the moving trains. The driver slumping over the accelerator, the train barely speeding up, the terrifyingly slow-motion derailment, the ridiculously minor injuries. The clean-up costs and the story in the local newspaper.

'Can we go home and play video games now?' our sons ask.

We wonder, just for a second, how long it would take us to die if we threw ourselves in front of one of the trains. How many times we would need to be run over. How long we'd have to lie on the track. We imagine the confusion as the trains hit us again and again every few minutes, the slow realisation of what was happening, the spreading feeling of horror among the other passengers, the eventual screams.

We don't know whether we'd have the force of will, not to mention the patience, to wait it out.

Sex

We're teaching our sons about sex.

We'd rather not have to teach our sons about sex this soon, all things being equal. Our sons would probably rather not have to learn about sex from us right now. Possibly everyone would be a lot happier if the subject had never come up.

But we have a responsibility, we tell them, as we follow the tracks together through the fresh morning snow. If they don't learn it from us, they're going to learn it from their school friends and all the pornography.

The pornography is everywhere, waiting to ambush our sons. Possibly it's already ambushed some of them. We don't know how we're supposed to respond to all the pornography. Obviously, we have fairly rudimentary responses to some of it. We're not saints.

But the sheer quantity, the scale, makes us feel dizzy.
And old.

'Well,' say the dads among us who actually perform in pornographic films, 'yes, but …'

'Sorry,' we say, 'we didn't mean to –'

'No, no,' they say, looking hurt, 'don't mind us trying to earn a living, trying to provide for our sons. It's fine.'

Obviously, it isn't fine. But, come on, nobody forced them into the business.

The divorced and separated and widowed dads among us, of course, have their own take on things. They're back on the market, whether they want to be or not, after years out of circulation. They all have thousand-yard stares, like men who have been under shellfire.

'It's all different now,' they tell us.

We stop by a silver birch tree, its branches heavy with a month's worth of snowfall.

'Different how?'

'Everyone has more choice than they know what to do with. More choice and more expectations. And less hair. Nobody is expected to have any hair anywhere any more.'

We know about the hair. Everyone knows about the hair.

'The hair thing has been going on for a while,' we explain to our sons.

We don't know how we feel about the hair thing. These days, we realise, we tend to look at women's bodies with a combination of nervousness and awe. Particularly the bodies of the mothers of our sons. We've seen what those bodies can do, what they can take. We've watched them carry and give birth to and nurture children.

We try not to think of women's bodies – and, in particular, the bodies of the mothers of our sons – as sexy warzones, sexy former battlefields, because it doesn't seem all that respectful.

But there we are.

We wonder how useful any of this is going to be to the gay sons.

'Oh, you have no idea,' say the gay dads.

But the snow has started falling again, muffling our voices, turning the world back to white, and we promised the mothers of our sons that we'd all be back in time for lunch.

Plane Crashes

We're teaching our sons about plane crashes.

We're teaching them how plane crashes happen, how to avoid or survive being in one. We're teaching them that plane crashes are incredibly rare, that the chances of experiencing a plane crash on a commercial airliner are approximately five million to one. We're teaching our sons that, no matter what they've seen on the internet, flying is far safer than driving, than travelling by train, than riding a bicycle.

Nevertheless, by the time the plane climbs to thirty-five thousand feet, we've already taken the emergency codeine we've been saving for exactly this sort of situation.

We've seen those plane crash films on the internet. We know all about shoe bombs, and anti-aircraft missiles, and iced-up pitot tubes, and wind shear, and thunderstorms, and botched inspections, and pilot error. We know how easy it is to unzip the thin aluminium tube we're sitting in; how much time we'd have to think about our fate as we fell through the frozen air, to think about the fate of our sons.

Our sons aren't scared of flying. They're excited about being allowed to do nothing but watch inflight movies for six or seven hours. They point down at the glorious crimson cloud tops, at the ships on the sea, don't even notice the bumps of random turbulence that cause us to clench our jaws.

We don't want to look out of the window.

We tell our sons about Antoine de Saint-Exupéry, who wrote *The Little Prince*, and who mysteriously disappeared while flying a reconnaissance mission in an unarmed P-38 during the Second World War. Antoine de Saint-Exupéry, whose father died before young Antoine's fourth birthday.

Our sons haven't read *The Little Prince*, haven't even heard of it.

'What are they teaching you these days?' we ask.

Our sons put their headphones back on. We know what their teachers are teaching them. They're teaching them to be better people.

Come to think of it, we haven't read *The Little Prince* either.

We stay awake all night, listening for slight changes in the tone of the engines, for the sounds of structural failure in the airframe, for sudden announcements of catastrophe. We stare down at the lights of cities, watch for panic on the faces of the cabin crew.

We keep pressing the call button to get the attention of the cabin crew.

'There was a noise,' we say.

The cabin crew just smile, tell us everything is going to be okay, give us more complimentary drinks.

Our sons, more used to living in the permanent present than we are, alternately sleep or watch cartoons, magnificently unaware of all the disasters that life has planned for them.

The best we can do, we realise, is to keep their hearts from breaking for as long as possible.

The Big Bang

We're teaching our sons about the Big Bang.

We're teaching them about the beginning of space-time, and the birth of the cosmos, and the origins of everything. We're explaining how reality as we know it probably expanded, by accident, from an infinitely small singularity, on borrowed energy that will eventually have to be paid back. We're trying to make it clear that we're all potentially the result of a single overlooked instance of cosmological miscounting.

Somehow, we've come on a stag do to Amsterdam with our sons in tow.

It's not going well.

It's late in the year and Amsterdam is spectacularly beautiful. Along the Herengracht the low afternoon light paints the tall houses in colours that take our breath away. In the Rijksmuseum, the Vermeers and Rembrandts seem to glow from within. On Keizersgracht the most beautiful women in the world ride past us on vintage bicycles.

But whatever way you look at it, this is no place for fathers to bring their sons.

The older sons want to sneak off and look in the windows of the brothels and hang around outside the sex shows, and the younger ones keep being nearly run over by all the beautiful cyclists.

'How was the world made?' the younger sons ask us. 'How did this all be true? Even before the olden days?'

We try to explain about false vacuums and the weak anthropic principle, about Higgs fields and the arrow of time, but it's no good. Half the dads have already been out to a coffee shop 'for a coffee', and the other half are waiting for their turn.

'But what about even before then?' the younger sons ask us. 'What was there before the bang?'

'Well, before then ... there wasn't really a then for things to be before.'

Nobody is convinced by that. We don't blame them. This whole trip was a terrible idea.

A group of the dads has got lost. The combination of all the weed and the conversation about primordial nucleosynthesis in the first seconds of the universe has tipped them over the edge. We send out a search party, roam the beautiful Golden Age streets. We keep getting invited into sex shows, decline politely.

After a couple of hours, we find the missing dads standing in a row outside the windows of a brothel, stoned, staring, confused, at the women in the windows.

We gently guide them away, apologise to everyone.

We haven't even started on the drinking competitions.

Ex-Girlfriends

We're teaching our sons about our ex-girlfriends.

How many of them there have been. What they meant to us. Where it all went wrong, again and again.

We turn up at the doors of our ex-girlfriends with our sons in tow, ask if we can come in and state our cases.

Our sons sit on the sofa, accept offers of juice and biscuits and say 'please' and 'thank you', are generally a credit to us. Our ex-girlfriends entertain the thought, just for a couple of seconds, that we have borrowed or stolen these children in order to impress them. That we are up to our old ways.

We are not up to our old ways.

We are aware of the remarkableness of our ex-girlfriends. We know we are lucky men to have loved and lost such spectacular and interesting women, to be in a position now to try to make amends for all our terrible behaviour.

Our ex-girlfriends are not so easily convinced.

'What are you doing here?' they ask. 'What is this about?'

'We're trying to make amends,' we say, 'having undertaken a searching and fearless moral inventory of ourselves. We want to make up for all the bad things we did back when we were drinking/gambling/on drugs/addicted to sex. For the lies, the betrayals, the constant unreliability, etc.'

Our ex-girlfriends are surprised.

'You were addicted to sex?' they ask.

'Well, no,' we say. 'It's just an example.'

'Right. Because we probably would have noticed.'

'Yes.'

Our ex-girlfriends think about it, remembering. Maybe for a bit longer than we're comfortable with.

'Now, Steve,' they say, '*he* was definitely addicted to sex.'

Everyone is quiet for a bit then. Our sons shift their gaze from us to our ex-girlfriends and back again. We had expected this to go differently, if we're honest. Outside the windows the late October light slowly fails.

'Well, anyway,' our ex-girlfriends say, eventually, 'it was all such a long time ago.'

They see us to the door, thank us for coming, tell our sons what fine young men they are, wish us all the best for the future.

Our sons look at us, about to say what we're all thinking.

'Who's Steve?' they ask.

The Loneliness of Billionaires

We're teaching our sons about the loneliness of billionaires.

We're explaining to our sons that the billionaires all live in exclusive penthouse apartments or isolated mansions or on their own private islands. On the beaches of their own private islands, we tell our sons, the billionaires weep. Because they don't have to worry about money, we explain, the billionaires worry about everything else.

They worry about the future, about population growth and disease, about how to save the world from climate change or the possibility that computers might one day become sentient and enslave mankind.

The billionaires are crushed by this terrible responsibility.

'Who would want to be a billionaire?' we ask our sons.

'Not us!' our sons all shout.

The billionaires spend their days inventing rockets and self-driving cars and supersonic trains. They hold competitions to find the best solutions to the world's most pressing problems. Our sons enter the competitions and win all-expenses-paid trips to meet the billionaires on their private islands.

As our seaplanes come in low over the island, the sun breaks through the clouds. The billionaires stand on the beaches in white linen trousers, waving to us. The sea is the deepest blue that any of us have ever seen, the beaches are the whitest white.

'Who would want to be a billionaire?' we ask.

Our sons nod, not really listening to us, thinking about it.

The billionaires put us up in grass-roofed lodges that face onto the white beaches, and we listen to the surf as we fall asleep. In the mornings when we wake up our sons are already walking along the beach, deep in conversation with the lonely billionaires.

We spend our days learning how to windsurf and going spearfishing while our sons work on top secret important projects. In the evenings the staff serve us baked sea bass at long tables on the beach, and we watch the sun go down and wait for our sons to join us. The clouds along the horizon are lit up like the end of the world, and our sons are always late for dinner. We start smoking again because we have nothing better to do, consider our stalled careers, think about the compromises we've made.

We wonder what we might have done with all the opportunities that our sons have been handed.

On the last night of our stay a fire breaks out in the big house at the end of the island. The big house is where the billionaires sleep, where they come up with their paradigm-shifting inventions, where they hold their transatlantic business meetings. We've never been allowed to visit the big house. Whenever we try to get a glimpse of what goes on in there we're run off by armed guards in dune buggies.

As the flames chew their way through the tropical hardwood of the big house, the billionaires stagger from the burning porch. Flames roll along the roof, climb the walls. The sky is dancing with glowing embers and ash.

The billionaires sink to their knees on the beaches. In their hands they hold the burned, sodden blueprints and plans. All those inventions. All those rockets and cars and trains.

'It's all ruined!' they shout, sobbing. 'Everything is ruined!'

In the dark, staring at the weeping billionaires, we pull our traumatised sons closer to us, hold their heads to our chests.

'Now do you see?' we whisper to them.

In the back pockets of our new white linen trousers, we can feel the slight weight of the cigarette lighter.

We decide we can live with the guilt.

Crying

We're teaching our sons about crying.

We're teaching them that it's okay to cry, that everyone cries, that men, by all accounts, should cry more. The consensus, we tell them, is that crying is mostly good.

Nevertheless, our sons complain that they've never seen us cry.

'Well, no …' we admit.

They've got us there. We've never cried in front of our sons.

We're not sure how we feel about this. We've only seen our own fathers cry once. We don't know whether or not it did us any good. At the time, we weren't sure how we were supposed to react. We don't know how we'd react now.

'We cried when you were born,' we tell our sons. 'We sobbed. We howled. There was no stopping us. For weeks afterwards we kept bursting into tears roughly every two hours.'

'Where did you cry?' our sons ask.

'We cried *everywhere*,' we tell them.

It's true. In the weeks after our sons were born we wept uncontrollably. We cried in supermarkets, on trains and buses, while brushing our teeth. We cried in car parks and lifts and corridors. We cried at the controls of cranes and armoured personnel carriers and nuclear power stations. We cried while holding our wives and partners, while performing surgery, while taking part in high-speed car chases, while playing in Premier League football matches. We cried while selling advertising space over the phone and while juggling knives in variety acts. We cried while delivering the mail, while working in Vietnamese restaurants, while plastering ceilings, while reading the ten o'clock news. We cried while trying to persuade people to help us liberate thousands of pounds from failed African states, while changing tractor tyres, while listening to motivational speeches. We cried at conferences, and at boxing matches, and at meetings of Alcoholics Anonymous and Gamblers Anonymous and Narcotics Anonymous. We cried in government and on the international space station and at the South Pole and in submarines at the bottom of the Marianas Trench. We cried during charity parachute jumps and driving tests and court cases. We cried while performing in pornographic films and while lecturing in particle physics. We cried in job centres and on cross-Channel ferries and while taking out the bins.

Partly, we suppose, it was the lack of sleep. Everything was raw. We felt like we'd been torn open to the world, and there was nothing we could do to stop it all from getting in.

'So what happened?' our sons ask.

'Eventually we had to get on with our lives,' we say. 'We couldn't just spend all day sitting around crying. Can you imagine what the world would be like?'

Our sons think about this, imagine us weeping from morning until night.

And we think about what we'd give, God, what we'd give to be able to feel that way again.

Europe

We're teaching our sons about Europe.

The size of it. The shape of it. How much of it is theirs.

We're driving around Europe marvelling at examples of the continent's rich history and magnificent infrastructure, its museums and art galleries and national parks. We're gazing in wonder at roads and airports and railways and bridges.

We drive across the breathtaking Ponte Vasco da Gama bridge in Portugal and think about the future of the European project. We drive across the breathtaking Viaduc de Millau bridge and the breathtaking Pont de Normandie bridge in France. We drive across the breathtaking Øresundsbroen bridge between Denmark and Sweden, across the breathtaking Sunnibergbrücke bridge in Switzerland.

'You can tell a lot about a country from its bridges,' we explain to our sons.

In the back of the car our sons are alternately well behaved and irritable. There are fights, travel sickness. We're asking a lot of them, we know. We've been travelling for a long time.

We tell our sons the story of Europe, all the way from the ice age up until the present day. Our sons are impressed by the scale of the bloodshed, the logistics of it all. They want to hear about the Thirty Years' War and the Eighty Years' War and the Hundred Years' War. They ask to visit castles and look at replica trebuchets and torture chambers. They refuse to be excited by coastal land reclamation or the single currency.

We take our sons to visit the Lascaux caves in south-western France, to see the Palaeolithic cave paintings. The paintings were created by some of the first Europeans, almost twenty thousand years ago. There are paintings of bulls, bison, lions, horses, rhinoceros, stags. Everybody is impressed with the craftsmanship; with the way the artists have managed to capture the essence of their animal subjects.

Nobody knows why the paintings were created, we tell our sons – whether it was to help guarantee successful hunts, or to celebrate them, or as an aid for ice-age fathers to teach their sons about their place in the world.

Our sons consider all this, quietly, think about their own places in the world, ask themselves what Europe means. We put our hands on their shoulders, proudly.

We don't have the heart to tell them that the whole thing is a fibreglass fake, that the real Lascaux caves have been closed since 1963 to preserve the fragile paintings from being damaged by the breath of the millions of people who visit every year.

We don't think they would appreciate the irony.

Empathy

We're teaching our sons about empathy.

We're teaching them how to share, how to consider other people's feelings, how to appreciate someone else's point of view. We're having mixed success. Sometimes it feels like we're raising hyenas.

The younger sons have been waging a guerrilla war against their older brothers for the last few months. They want their own rooms, want their older brothers to move out – although there's nowhere for them to go. Their methods of asymmetrical warfare include sabotage, the use of booby traps, midnight ambushes, and pre-dawn hit-and-run raids.

The older brothers are starting to show signs of battle fatigue. They're becoming jumpy and hollow-eyed. They refuse to go to the bathroom without checking for tripwires first, sleep with their nerf guns loaded and ready by their sides.

'Why do you have to fight with your brothers all the time?' we ask the younger sons.

'The revolution is not an apple that falls when it is ripe,' they tell us. 'You have to make it fall.'

'What does that mean?'

'They started it.'

We try to bring both sides to the negotiating table for peace talks. The peace talks are held over breakfast. The younger sons come with a list of demands. They've taken to wearing headbands, to holding classes on revolutionary thought in the back garden. We have to ask them to stop referring to their older brothers as 'The Oppressor'.

'You see what we have to put up with?' the older brothers say.

'They keep punching us!' our younger sons claim, indignant.

'Please don't punch your brothers,' we say.

We draw up an agreement for the sharing of toys and the rights to any exploitable natural resources between the bunk beds and the wardrobe, get the younger sons to agree to temporarily suspend their Christmas bombing campaign.

'Remember that the true revolutionary is guided by a great feeling of love,' we tell them. 'It is impossible to think of a genuine revolutionary lacking this quality.'

Our sons nod, stand their forces down. Both sides withdraw to consider their positions. For two days an uneasy peace reigns.

Until the morning we wake up to hear them whispering to each other through the wall, and spot the pillow barricades by their door, the toy guns aimed at our bedroom, and feel too late the sharp twang of the wire as we step onto the landing.

Haunted Houses

We're teaching our sons about haunted houses.

We're taking them on explorations of abandoned lunatic asylums and ruined stately homes and spooky hotels where the corridors go on for miles. We're spending the night in deserted mansions, armed only with torches and sleeping bags.

'What was that?' our sons ask, sitting up in the dark, in their *Paw Patrol-* and Pokemon-themed sleeping bags.

We tell them it was only the wind, the sound of the old house settling, mice under the floorboards.

'Go back to sleep,' we say.

We're fairly certain it wasn't mice under the floorboards. Not just mice, anyway.

'Tell us a story,' our sons ask, 'to help take our minds off all the terrifying things that could potentially be hiding in the dark.'

So we tell our sons how we used to play in the garden of the local deserted mansion when we were children, how we would climb over the wall of the overgrown orchard, throw stones at the broken windows, dare each other to climb the stone steps and knock on the front door.

We tell them about the time when we stayed too late one evening and saw the girl's pale face at the window as the sky filled with swooping bats. How she haunted our dreams for years afterwards.

'Who was she?' our sons whisper. 'Did she live there?'

'Nobody lived there,' we say, and we realise we haven't thought about any of this since we were twelve years old. 'Nobody had lived there since before we were born.'

We all sit there listening to the creaking of the trees outside the window, the rise and fall of our breath.

Eventually our sons yawn.

'Great story, Dad,' they say, and roll over and shut their eyes.

Our sons go to sleep and we stay awake until the sun comes up, watching the corners of the room, waiting for the impossible return of everything we've ever lost.

Relationships

We're teaching our sons about relationships.

We're teaching them how to have relationships, and what relationships are for, and what to do and what to avoid doing in them.

We're all in McDonald's on a Saturday morning, mainly on account of the divorced and separated and widowed dads. It's practically their second home.

When we were younger, we explain to our sons, we thought that relationships were supposed to solve all your problems. We thought that all you had to do was to get someone to fall in love with you and you'd suddenly be handed the life you'd always wanted. That you would suddenly, somehow, become the person you'd always wanted to be.

Consequently, we tell our sons, all our relationships tended to end the same way: in heartbreak and despair and things getting set on fire.

Our sons, elbows deep in their Happy Meals, nod knowingly.

Now things are different, we tell them. Now we understand that what relationships actually do is provide you with a whole new set of problems to deal with, so you don't have time to worry about all the stupid, self-indulgent stuff you used to worry about before.

In this way, we say, relationships are not unlike children.

'Relationships, above all, are work,' we tell our sons, as we all leave McDonald's and head towards the park.

'But nobody gets paid,' our sons remind us.

'No.'

The divorced and separated and widowed fathers are simultaneously a lot more optimistic and a lot more cynical than the rest of us in their view of relationships. They've been around the block, they remind us all, dragging on their cigarettes – the cigarettes that they only started smoking again when they got divorced or separated or their partners died. They've built relationships only to watch them crumble or blow apart or collapse like dying stars, on account of one or both parties having sex with other people, or wanting to have sex with other people, or growing up, or not growing up, or getting bored, or dying tragically young.

Nevertheless, the divorced and separated and widowed fathers tell us, they're still willing to get back on the horse.

Because what else is there?

We go with the divorced and separated and widowed fathers to watch them get haircuts and makeovers and body waxes. They take us for rides in their sports cars and introduce us to their new girlfriends and prospective girlfriends, who are all as lovely as you would expect. The older prospective girlfriends, who have been down this road before and have children of their own, are reserved with us but great with our sons.

Somewhere across town, we imagine, their ex-husbands are likely sitting in other, similar branches of McDonald's, having much the same conversations as the rest of us.

Mountains

We're teaching our sons about mountains.

We're teaching them how to approach mountains, how to understand mountains, how to classify mountains, how to climb mountains. We're trying to get our sons to understand what mountains mean to us, in exactly the same way that our fathers failed to get us to understand what mountains meant to them.

Together with our sons we're planning to climb the ten highest mountains on the planet. We're going to sit on the summits of the ten highest mountains on the planet and smoke cigarettes and watch the sun come up and ponder the sublime.

We'll have to take our oxygen masks off to smoke our cigarettes, root around inside our gigantic down jumpsuits for some matches or a lighter. Our starved red blood cells will wither in protest. Our lungs will howl.

From up there we'll be able to see the curvature of the earth, the thin orange line of the troposphere on the horizon, the stratosphere and mesosphere shading white into blue into the blackness of space.

'This is what you trained for,' we'll tell our sons. 'This is the reward for your sacrifice. Smoke your cigarette.'

So far our sons are unconvinced. They don't see the use of mountains, see even less point in climbing them. They want to watch TV or play with their friends.

We don't blame them. We felt exactly the same.

We tell ourselves that they'll thank us one day, as we drag them out of their beds before dawn every morning, make them eat their porridge, check their ropes and gear. We remind ourselves that even Beethoven had to be forced to practise the piano every day as a child, weeping at the pain in his bruised fingers, the cuts that never healed.

Was it Beethoven or was it Mozart?

One day, we tell ourselves, it will all be worth it.

Drugs

We're teaching our sons about drugs.

What they do, why people take them, where to find them.

For the last six weeks we've been travelling up the Amazon river in search of mind-expanding experiences. Under the expert teaching of local shamans we've been ingesting potions made from magical tree bark and smoking the leaves of incredibly rare vines and drinking the venom of critically endangered spiders and snakes.

We're looking for answers to the questions we've been asking ourselves all of our lives.

Our sons are being remarkably patient. In the evenings they swim with pink river dolphins and eat fish for dinner. Then they have their bedtime stories, scoot down under their mosquito nets, sleep soundly under skies filled with giant wheeling stars.

While we journey the vast and terrifying reaches of the universe, guided only by unreliable spirit animals.

In the afternoons it rains in the jungle, and the rain sounds like the end of days. Our sons draw cartoons in the long house, play with the local kids, catch scorpions and bullet ants. We ask the local shamans if enlightenment is always this long coming, if it has to involve so much throwing up.

'Direct your question to the jaguar,' the shamans tell us. 'Direct your question to the monkey.'

To be honest, we're getting sick of directing our questions to the jaguar and the monkey. And the cayman and the piracu and the mighty anaconda and the giant centipede and the vampire bat.

None of them ever gives us a straight answer.

Our sons send emails home to their mothers and their schoolmates, tell stories of tarantulas as big as dinner plates, and the family of wild pigs that they've adopted, and the smell of the trees after the rain. They have their faces painted with ink made with ashes from the fire, learn how to make bows and arrows and blow pipes, go on hunting trips for monkeys and birds.

And every day they travel a little bit further into the jungle without us, come back a little bit nearer dark.

The shamans, who have likely had enough of us now, tell us about another village, further up the river, beyond the falls, where the locals chew the hallucinogenic leaves of a tree so rare it grows nowhere else on earth. There, they tell us, we might find what we're looking for.

Our sons, carefully coating the tips of their arrows with poison, volunteer to stay behind until our return.

The Bradford Goliath

We're teaching our sons about the Bradford Goliath.

Who he was. What he represented. Why we'll never forget him.

When we were growing up, we explain to our sons, our next door neighbour Gary's dad was a bodybuilder. He was huge. Three children could hang off each of his arms. He ate six raw eggs for breakfast every morning and did two hundred press-ups in the middle of the street before 8 a.m. He spent all day lifting weights in a caravan that he'd parked in front of the house.

He was in training to become The World's Strongest Man.

'How did he get so strong?' our sons ask. 'What was his job?'

'He didn't have a job,' we tell our sons. 'He'd been on the sick from the electricity board ever since being electrocuted while servicing a sub-station. He'd been clinically dead for ten minutes. When he regained consciousness he discovered he was permanently deaf in one ear and had the strength of ten men. It was a miracle.'

To supplement his sick pay, we explain, Gary's dad started performing feats of strength at outdoor exhibitions. Wearing a wrestling mask and a leotard he would rip planks of wood in half and pull tractors with his teeth and blow up hot water bottles like balloons until they burst. He became famous across West Yorkshire as 'The Bradford Goliath'.

And he was ours.

'By the month of the World's Strongest Man televised final,' we tell our sons, 'Gary's dad was pumping iron round the clock and getting through six steaks and three roast chickens a day. After a near-riot by the other customers he was banned from the local butcher's. It was the hottest summer since 1976, and tempers were short.

'And then, one day during the holidays, when we were all playing out in the street, we heard that horrible noise from the caravan.'

He'd never really had a chance, of course. The same accident that had given him superpowers had made him ineligible for the competition. Heart attack. Clinically dead for ten minutes. There was no way they would risk him in front of a worldwide audience.

It should have been obvious, if he'd ever stopped to think

about it. Nobody wants to see The World's Strongest Man drop dead on television.

They could have sent the rejection letter earlier though.

'He tore through the aluminium walls of the caravan like they were paper,' we tell our sons, 'bigger than any of us could have imagined a man to be. He was Godzilla. He was King Kong. He blocked out the sun and could not be stopped. He kicked down the front door of his house and the TV came flying out through the window, then the settee, the kitchen table, the bath. By the time he emerged from the wreckage a crowd had gathered. When he strode into the middle of the road and roared, the shockwave broke kitchen windows all down the street.'

In the end it took a police marksman with a sniper rifle and a magazine full of tranquilliser darts to stop him. Apparently the bill for the damage to the street nearly bankrupted the council. They had to haul him onto the back of a lorry with a crane.

'And as they drove him away past the overturned cars and the uprooted lamp posts,' we continue, 'all the men took off their hats and all the women bowed their heads in respect.'

Our sons digest this, trying to work out a moral, a message from it.

And all this time later, we realise, we're still trying to do the same.

Gambling

We're teaching our sons about gambling.

It's four in the morning and we're on the terrace of the Monte Carlo Casino, drinking cocktails and looking wistfully out across the dark blue Mediterranean Sea.

We're waiting for the sun to come up.

Our sons have had enough; they want to go to bed. They wanted to go to bed hours ago. They're slumped against the magnificent wrought-iron railings of the terrace of the Monte Carlo Casino, wishing they were at home.

No one is exactly sure how we all got in here – where we got all the tuxedos from, who gave us our stake. Aren't there supposed to be rules about/against this sort of thing?

'Who's actually paying for all of this?' we ask.

The divorced and separated fathers look sheepish. This is exactly the sort of caper that led to them getting divorced and separated in the first place. This is why we don't go out drinking with the divorced and separated fathers that much any more.

'Just one more bet,' they say. 'Just one more spin of the wheel. Just one more roll of the dice. There's still a chance to turn everything around.'

We decide we need to get the divorced and separated fathers out of there, take them down to the beach to sober up. We end up walking along a busy road with our half-asleep sons in tow, stretched out behind us like ducklings as the sky starts to colour, trying to avoid getting run over by all the Ferraris and Bugattis and Porsches heading back home from the nightclubs.

On the beach our sons fall asleep under our coats in the shadow of the multi-storey apartment blocks and hotels. Every few minutes the police drive past to check we're not up to anything. The first of the day's joggers have already started up along the sea front.

'Don't they realise it isn't tomorrow yet?' say the divorced and separated fathers, swigging from the bottles of Krug that they've liberated from the bar of the casino. 'Don't they know it's still last night?'

'How much did you lose?' we ask.

'Everything!' the divorced and separated fathers laugh. 'We lost everything.'

'No, we meant –'

'We know what you meant.'

Out on the dark blue Mediterranean Sea breakfast is being served on the super yachts. Their champagne finished, the divorced and separated fathers lie down next to their sons, try to snuggle up under their coats with them.

We hope somebody knows what time the flights are.

It's already tomorrow.

Food

We're teaching our sons about food.

How to cook and eat it. The importance of it. What it has meant to people through the ages.

We're putting our sons to work as pot-washers and kitchen porters and trainee commis chefs in restaurant kitchens and hospital kitchens and the kitchens of cruise ships and prisons. It's clearly ridiculous – our sons are far too young for this sort of thing. And there are obvious legal issues to consider.

Nevertheless.

'It's important to have a trade,' we say cheerfully, as we wave our sons off for the summer.

On the rolling seas or in the back streets of the world's capital cities or during prison riots our sons learn how to handle knives and bain-maries and Hobart-brand industrial dishwashers, how to survive serious burns and the loss of fingertips, how to manage having their hearts broken by beautiful and doomed waitresses/waiters.

It never did us any harm. Just look at us, for God's sake.

When they come back home at the end of the summer our sons are taciturn and reserved. They don't want to talk about their experiences, don't want to share with us what they've learned. To be fair, they're like this when they come home from school, too.

To make up for what we've put them through, we try to take our sons to visit The Greatest Restaurant in the World.

The Greatest Restaurant in the World is high in the Pyrenees. It's a two-hour bus ride from the airport. The view is spectacular but there's a ten-year waiting list for a table. There's no way we're getting in.

We point out the famous singers and politicians and busi-nessmen and businesswomen eating octopus sashimi and pressed duck on the terrace, the millionaires and billionaires drinking fifty-year-old wine and one-hundred-year-old brandy. Then we sneak round to the back door, where the kitchen staff smuggle free samples from the taster menu out to us.

'Never forget you are the finest of men,' the kitchen staff tell our sons, raising their fists in solidarity.

Our sons return the salute, look at the heroic kitchen staff the way they used to look at us, and we recognise too late the terrible mistake that we've made.

The Life-Saving Properties of Books

We're teaching our sons about the life-saving properties of books.

We tell our sons about the books that saved our lives when we were fourteen, and about the books that saved our lives again when we were sixteen, and about the books that saved our lives again when we were eighteen, and about the books that saved our lives again when we were twenty-one and thirty-five.

We've prepared lists for our sons of books that might help them in any number of different, life-threatening situations.

'What were you doing that your lives needed saving so often?' our sons ask, taking the lists and folding them up and putting them in their back pockets.

It's a fair question.

All the libraries in the country are being shut down because there's no money left. We take our sons to the protests at their local library and listen to poetry readings and speeches. There are fun, creative things for the children to do, things to cut apart and things to stick back together again. There are professional children's entertainers who are giving up their time for free and who teach our sons how to make balloon animals.

'When we were your age,' we whisper to our sons, 'your grandmothers were librarians. They used to let us play in the library after closing time. In the dark, the shelves seemed to go on for miles. It was like being lost in a forest of books.'

We go to visit the grandmothers and they tell our sons about their adventures in the library trade. They tell stories of mobile libraries, and of floating libraries on canal barges, and of libraries on cruise ships and trans-continental trains, and of flying libraries in the Australian outback, and of caravans of libraries in the Sahara desert, and of old-fashioned horse-drawn libraries bringing the gift of education to the masses in the days before the war, and of ice libraries dug out of glaciers in the French Alps, and of isolated mountaintop libraries in China tended by Buddhist monks, and of futur-istic underwater libraries, and of libraries in space, and of guerrilla libraries in the tunnels beneath occupied cities, their books coated with the dust that falls from the ceilings every time a bomb hits, and of cursed libraries in caves, and of fabulous lost libraries deep in the Amazon jungle, and of evil libraries constructed in the craters of extinct volcanoes, and

of lovers' libraries full of the most romantic books ever writ-
ten, and of magical libraries that only appear at certain times
of the year, and of the libraries at the South Pole, and of
illegal libraries containing nothing but banned books, and of
legendary, metaphorical libraries that go on for ever.

'No books were ever out of bounds to you,' the grand-
mothers remind us, as our sons browse their dusty
bookshelves.

And it's true. We were allowed to read whatever we
wanted. Even the books that terrified us so much we didn't
sleep for weeks afterwards.

We decide it's time to get going, quickly remove all those
potentially terrifying books from our sons' hands. Because
there are more protests to go to. Because those libraries aren't
going to save themselves.

Actually, most of the time it's our sons' mothers who take
them to the library protests, but the point we're trying to
make still stands.

Crime

We're teaching our sons about crime.

We're teaching them that crime doesn't pay, or that *mostly* it doesn't pay, or that, in fact, it can sometimes pay quite handsomely.

It's all a matter of perspective, we explain. It all depends on who you ask.

Statistically, with this many dads, it's inevitable that some of us will be criminals. We likely include forgers and fraudsters, con men, bank robbers, jewel thieves, sellers of stolen goods, loan sharks, burglars, muggers, importers of contraband cigarettes, football hooligans, people smugglers, arms dealers, owners of pyramid and Ponzi schemes, hit men, drunk drivers, dog-fight organisers, corrupt council officials, money launderers, and medium-to-high-level drug dealers.

Or worse.

And we either want to teach our sons the family business, to pass on to them our smoothly functioning and highly lucrative criminal trades and gangland empires, or we're determined that they aren't going to follow in our footsteps. We're doing all of this (whatever it is that we're doing, we're evasive on this point) to ensure that our wonderful sons will never have to.

The criminal dads assemble everyone, fathers and sons, in lock-up garages. They set up interactive whiteboards, walk us all through *the job*. This is where we enter the building, they explain. This is where we land the boats on the beach. This is where the crooked security guard is paid to look the other way. This is where we cut the wires to the alarm system. This is where we move the decimal point without anyone noticing.

'What about guard dogs?' our sons ask. 'What about the time lock on the vault? What about witnesses? What about the taxman?'

The criminal dads are impressed. They look away, briefly choked up. It's a proud moment for all of us.

'And what's the cardinal rule?' the criminal dads ask.

'Snitches get stitches!' our sons chant in unison.

Later, we'll promise to visit the criminal dads in prison, re-dedicate ourselves to raising their sons alongside our own as fine and upstanding citizens. We'll lift a drink to our fallen comrades, pour one out on the ground for them.

We won't tell our sons about our own brief and not so brief teenage shoplifting careers, our arrests for minor criminal trespass, our minor and not so minor drug offences.

We won't tell them how you used to be able to rob vending machines with four pieces of sellotape and a five-pound note (it doesn't work any more, they've changed the vending machines now, we've tried), we won't explain how to get into a locked car with a strip of plastic.

And yet.

We still know the blind spots of every security camera in our nearest shopping centre, and how to spot a store detective, and the likelihood of getting away with it at different times of the day on different days of the week. If you were in that sort of business.

Because nobody looks twice at a middle-aged dad.

And we like to keep our hands in.

Glaciers

We're teaching our sons about glaciers.

We're explaining how glaciers are formed, how they grow and retreat, how they've impacted landscapes and cultures around the world since the end of the last ice age. We're explaining about U-shaped valleys and truncated spurs and medial and terminal moraines, about Otzi the 5,000-year-old iceman who was discovered frozen in a glacier in the Austrian Alps. We tell our sons what would happen if all the water locked up in glaciers was released by global warming, how sea levels would rise by metres.

We go on a field trip to visit our nearest glacier. We stand on the edge of a crevasse and stare down into the endless blue depths, imagine what it would be like to fall in and be carried along in all that ice, travelling down the valley at a speed of roughly one thousand metres a year.

'Three hundred years ago,' we tell our sons, 'the glacier

reached all the way down to the village at the bottom of the valley. And every year it advanced a little bit further. Nothing could stop it. It destroyed crops, fields, even houses. People thought the glacier was possessed by the devil. That it was going to keep growing for ever, that eventually the whole world would be taken over by ice.'

'So what did they do?' our sons ask.

'They had an exorcism. They held a religious ceremony right at the front of the glacier and got the local priest to cast out the demons.'

'Did they have a human sacrifice?'

'Where did you learn about human sacrifice?' we ask.

Our sons shrug.

'School.'

'Maybe they sacrificed a goat or something. The Catholic Church wasn't very big on human sacrifices.'

'Did it work?'

'Well, sometime in the eighteenth century the glacier stopped advancing,' we tell them, 'and it's been shrinking ever since.'

It's true. In pictures from a hundred years ago the glacier is almost a mile further down the valley than it is now. We can even spot the change in the ten years since we were last here.

This is where we came with the mothers of our sons for our last big holiday before we became parents. We rode all the chairlifts and cable cars and went inside the hundred-metre-long cave they dig out of the glacier every summer and took pictures of each other against the walls of ice.

In the pictures the blue light filtering down through the ice makes it look like we're underwater. And we are so young.

They've started covering the surface of the glacier with carpet in the summer now to try to stop it melting away any faster. We wonder if that would work with our relationship with the mothers of our sons. If we'd fallen into a crevasse together on that trip, we realise, we'd still have a good forty or fifty years before we emerged, perfect and hand-in-hand, from the ice at the glacier front.

What Happens When You Get Struck by Lightning

We're teaching our sons about what happens when you get struck by lightning.

We're explaining that the earth is hit by a lightning strike approximately fifty times every second, that around a thousand people across the world are struck by lightning every day, that people struck by lightning have, roughly, a one in ten chance of dying.

For comparison, the chance of being killed by bees is roughly one in six million.

'Do you explode?' our sons ask. 'Do your eyes go on fire? Do flames shoot out of the ends of your fingers? Can people see your skeleton, just for a second?'

We're walking in the forest, spotting trees that have been hit by lightning. There are a surprisingly high number. We're beginning to wish we'd checked the weather before we came out. There's a definite ozone tang to the air, and the hairs on our arms are starting to stand up.

'You'd be likely to get very badly burnt,' we say, 'especially at the points where the lightning enters and exits your body. But you don't normally explode.'

'What about superpowers?' our sons ask. 'Can getting hit by lightning give you superpowers?'

We tell our sons that the after-effects of being hit by lightning can include mood swings, seizures, deafness, memory loss, changes in personality, headaches and chronic pain.

'Like having children, ha ha!'

We tell them that the best way to avoid being hit by lightning is not to be outside during a thunderstorm, to stay away from bodies of water and objects that conduct electricity – like fences and windmills. And trees. We tell them the story of Roy Sullivan, the American park ranger who held the record for being struck by lightning more times than any other human being. Between 1942 and 1977, we tell them, poor Roy Sullivan was struck by lightning on seven different occasions.

'Why did he get hit so many times?' our sons ask.

'Nobody knows,' we say, 'maybe he was just unlucky. He was a park ranger so he did spend a lot of time outdoors.'

'Maybe he was magnetic,' our sons say. 'Maybe he was somehow attracting the lightning. Maybe there was actually metal inside his bones and he didn't know it. Maybe *he was a robot.*'

'It's possible,' we say.

We remember reading about Roy Sullivan in the *Guinness Book of Records* when we were young, remember being touched by the fact that, after surviving seven separate lightning strikes in thirty-five years, he killed himself over an unrequited love affair at the age of seventy-one.

We still don't know whether to find this wildly romantic, ironic or absurd. We stop walking and turn to our sons, not sure, exactly, what the lesson is here.

And then we all hear the sound of thunder in the distance, and freeze.

The World's Most Dangerous Spiders

We're teaching our sons about the world's most dangerous spiders.

Where they live. The likelihood of being bitten by one. Their medical significance.

The world's most dangerous spiders are the Brazilian wandering spider (*Phoneutria nigriventer*), the Sydney funnel-web spider (*Atrax robustus*) and the black widow spider (*Latrodectus mactans*, and others). These spiders have all been responsible for numerous recorded deaths, although, with the development of antivenins, fatalities are very rare these days.

Other potentially dangerous spiders include the brown recluse spider, the yellow sac spider and the mouse spider. However, as none of these spiders live in northern Europe, we explain to our sons, there's very little to worry about.

'Tell us about the time our great-granddad fought a Brazilian wandering spider,' our sons ask.

So we tell them, again, the story of their great-grandfather's battle with the Brazilian wandering spider.

We tell them how their great-grandfather used to have a grocer's shop, where he sold fruit and vegetables and the odd rabbit. We tell them how, one morning, he opened a crate of imported bananas and suddenly found himself confronted by a highly aggressive spider that had accidentally hitched a ride all the way from Brazil. We describe the way the spider reared up in the characteristic warning posture, its front four legs held high to reveal its huge fangs. How it lunged at their great-grandfather. Their great-grandfather, who had survived the First World War despite being blown up and buried in a shell hole for three days and then catching malaria. Their great-grandfather, who was now facing the possibility of meeting his maker in this ludicrous manner, among the smell of overripe South American fruit.

'And what did he do?' our sons ask. They've never met their great-grandfather. He died thirty years before they were born. We hardly remember him ourselves, although in the pictures taken of him as a young man he looks exactly like us.

'What do you think he did?'

'He smashed the spider with the hammer he'd been using to open the banana crates!' our sons all shout.

'Exactly!' we say.

We don't know how many times we've told this story. Our fathers originally told it to us, except in those days nobody had heard of Brazilian wandering spiders, so the spider in the story was a tarantula. These days, tarantulas, as our sons are well aware, aren't considered to be dangerous at all. They're also unlikely to be found in crates of bananas.

The story works better, makes more sense with a Brazilian wandering spider. Possibly our sons will replace it with a different species of spider if they ever tell the story to their children. If they ever have children.

If there are still spiders by then.

As well as being one of the most dangerous spiders in the world, the Brazilian wandering spider is also famous for having a bite which causes men to have painful erections that can last for hours.

We don't tell our sons this.

We don't think it would add anything to the story.

Friendship

We're teaching our sons about friendship.

We're going away for a long weekend in the hills with the same group of male friends we've been going away with since we were teenagers. We explain to our sons that it's important to have relationships with people who've known you longer than you've known yourself. That it matters to be among people who have no expectations of you.

'Can we come with you?' our sons ask.

'No,' we tell them.

On the first day of the long weekend we all walk up a hill together, all the middle-aged and nearly middle-aged men. We briefly ask after each other's families, careers, cars and houses. We look at the sheep, take in the rainy views and the clean air.

Then we spend the evening and the next two days sitting around the rented cottage in our tracksuits, drinking and smoking and taking hallucinogenic drugs and having competitions to see who can do the most chin-ups or eat the most biscuits in one go.

Sometimes we go to the pub across the road.

We don't discuss our lives, or our worries, or our hopes for the future, or our fears of what happens next. We don't talk about our money problems or our health. At one point we invent a new version of indoor golf, briefly consider marketing it and becoming rich. We take it in turns to see who can climb to the top of the two-storey stone chimney in the double-height lounge.

Through the windows the endless rain washes the surface of the lake, day and night.

And nobody goes to bed.

Around dawn on the third day somebody notices that Kev has disappeared. We check to see whether he's fallen asleep in the bath or accidentally locked himself in the cellar. He's not in the house.

We all put on our boots and stagger outside in the grey half-light. We wander around the fields calling Kev's name and disturbing the sheep. The wet grass brushes our tracksuit bottoms. The soft rain falls on our faces.

Eventually we find Kev down by the lake, sitting on a rock, looking at pictures of his kids on his phone and crying softly to himself.

Nobody wants to see that.

'What's he taken?' someone asks. 'What have you taken, Kev?'

'We all took the same thing,' says someone else. 'Didn't we all take the same thing?'

We all stand around feeling uncomfortable while Kev sobs quietly. A breeze ruffles the surface of the lake. Eventually someone goes to the house and comes back with a cup of tea for Kev.

'Cup of tea, Kev mate,' they say.

'Thanks,' Kev says, sniffling. He wipes his eyes and gives everyone a weak smile. An embarrassed thumbs-up.

'I was just, y'know …' he indicates the hills, the sky, with a sweep of his arm. Holds up the phone with the pictures of his kids.

'Right,' we say. 'Yeah.'

Nobody says anything for a while after that. We smoke our cigarettes, look at the sheep, wonder if the clouds are ever going to clear from the top of the hills.

And then, awkwardly, one by one, we all clap Kev on the shoulder, before trooping back to the house, leaving Kev to pull himself together on his own, in his own time.

Single Mothers

We're teaching our sons about single mothers.

We're teaching them to respect, admire and look up to single mothers, particularly the single mothers of their friends and classmates, and to be in awe of their mysterious powers.

We're warning our sons not to cross the single mothers, not to mess them about, not to wind them up. We're reminding them to be on their best behaviour when they go round to the houses of their friends who are being raised by single mothers.

'Whatever you do,' we say, 'don't make them angry.'

The single mothers are all holding down three different jobs and studying for degrees and dealing with their children's complicated medical conditions and trying to bring up their sons and daughters as well-balanced and polite and confident young men and women.

They haven't got time for any nonsense from the likes of us.

Standing at the school gates and during school carol concerts and in the park on Sunday mornings we marvel at the single mothers. We're amazed by their toughness, their bravery, their terrifying improvisational skills.

'They can do anything,' say the fathers of the sons of the single mothers, somewhat sheepishly.

They're hoping this gets them off the hook.

'Can they do stunts?' our sons ask.

'Almost definitely,' we say.

'Could they jump off the top of a moving mine cart and grab on to a rope and swing across a river of lava?'

'If anyone could do that, it would be them.'

'Could they run down a corridor and keep ducking under a series of spinning blades while diving *over* sets of spikes that come up from the floor?'

'It wouldn't surprise us.'

'Could they be chased down a hill by a giant boulder and then go over a waterfall in a boat and still survive?'

'It's possible.'

'Could they –'

'Yes,' we say. 'Yes, they could.'

At the school gates and during school carol concerts and in the park on Sunday mornings the single mothers get on with things with their usual military precision. They eye us suspiciously, for the fractions of a second that their schedules allow.

We all try to stand or sit a little bit straighter, to look like better fathers.

We loudly remind our sons to have a good day or to just relax and enjoy the show or to not fall off the slide, to remember to drink their water, to always strive to be fine and upstanding citizens.

And we try to overhear what the single mothers are saying to their children.

We wonder what they're teaching their sons, what terrible secrets we could learn from them about being better men.

The Conquest of the South Pole

We're teaching our sons about the Conquest of the South Pole.

We're teaching them about Scott of the Antarctic, and the doomed Terra Nova Expedition, and the heroic Captain Oates walking out of the tent to die in a blizzard in order to give his comrades a better chance of making it home alive, and certain other forms of suicidal English male stoicism that we still find inspiring in spite of our better judgement.

We're teaching our sons about the considerable superiority of sled dogs over pit ponies as the animal of choice for a journey to the ends of the earth.

'What about polar bears?' our sons ask.

'There are no polar bears in the Antarctic,' we say. 'Only penguins and seals.'

'But could you train a polar bear to pull a sledge?'

'We don't –'

'The polar bears could also protect you from your enemies.'

'What enemies would anyone have at the South Pole?' we ask.

'Other explorers. People trying to steal your supplies. Your food.'

'Good point.'

'You couldn't eat the polar bears when they died though,' our sons remind us. 'Because polar bear liver contains lethal levels of vitamin A.'

'So it does.'

We don't tell our sons about The Worst Journey in the World, when three members of Scott's Antarctic expedition, including the writer Apsley Cherry-Garrard, spent a month travelling on foot across the continent through the endless polar night in order to collect unhatched emperor penguin eggs for scientific study. After barely surviving horrific blizzards, temperatures of minus 40 degrees, the loss of their tent and most of their teeth, the team eventually returned with just three intact eggs.

The eggs are still in the Natural History Museum in London.

We don't tell our sons that Cherry-Garrard never really recovered from the journey, or from what he saw as his personal failure to save Scott's team from starving to death on their return from the pole. We don't tell them about the book that he wrote recounting the journey and its aftermath, which contains the most devastating last line we've ever read.

Inevitably, we wonder how we would have survived in those conditions, how long it would have taken us to give up and surrender. We hope that we would have been inspired to keep going by thinking about our sons, by our determination to see them again.

But then, loving our sons, we don't know how we would have found ourselves that far away from them in the first place.

Of Scott's team, Edgar Evans, who died on the return from the pole, had three children. Scott had a son, who was only two when his father died.

Cherry-Garrard, who survived to return to England, get invalided out of the First World War and write his book, never had children. He spent most of his life suffering from chronic depression.

In the event, the eggs that he and his comrades collected added little to the sum of scientific knowledge.

Monsters

We're teaching our sons about monsters.

We're teaching them how to correctly identify zombies, vampires and werewolves, how to avoid or defend themselves against them. How to most effectively kill them, if it comes to that.

We're hanging around in graveyards and crypts, on lonely moonlit moors, outside the gates of apparently abandoned castles.

Naturally, our sons are arguing amongst themselves about the finer details.

'Werewolves don't just kill you – they turn you into were-wolves as well. If you get killed by a werewolf, you come back as a werewolf too.'

'No, that's vampires. You only turn into a werewolf if you *survive* a werewolf attack.'

'Vampires don't turn you into a vampire. They just drink your blood.'

'If a vampire drinks nearly all your blood but you don't die and then they give you some of their own blood then you become one of the living dead like them.'

'Zombies are the living dead, not vampires. Vampires are the undead.'

'If a zombie bites you, you die and *then* you turn into a zombie and come back to life. But as a zombie.'

'What would happen if a vampire got bitten by a zombie?'

'A zombie wouldn't bite a vampire – they only bite people who are alive.'

'Could you have a zombie werewolf? Or a werewolf vampire?'

'What's the difference between a skeleton and a zombie?'

Etc.

We wonder if this is an altogether healthy conversation. It is exactly the kind of thing that we used to discuss with our friends and brothers when we were young, but then, look at us. We're the sort of men who take their sons wandering through graveyards and across lonely moors and up to the gates of abandoned castles in the middle of the night.

We're nowhere near being the sort of fine people that we hope our sons will become.

And yet we also know that this is the kind of knowledge that most of the mothers of our sons can't pass on. Given the situation, would they even know how best to employ a hawthorn stake or silver bullets or a sharpened spade, and which monsters to use them against?

We would. And, surely, that has to count for something.

The media is reporting that a child has disappeared on the way home from school on the edge of a town a hundred miles away. It's so rare an occurrence, thank God, that the disappearance is the lead story. An entire village has been mobilised to look for the boy. Everyone is holding their breath. Nobody wants to think about how these things end.

At some point, we know, we'll need to talk to our sons about those kinds of monsters, too.

But not yet. Please, not yet.

Romance

We're teaching our sons about romance.

We're explaining about romantic songs and books and poetry, about romantic poets with romantic diseases, about how romance has very little to do with the real, tough, day-to-day business of love.

'For the most part,' we tell our sons, 'romance makes people do stupid and desperate things. It makes them lie and cheat and steal and invade other countries and blow things up. For the most part,' we say, 'romance is not to be trusted.'

Our sons nod. They like the bit about stuff getting blown up. They've got no interest, not yet, in romance.

'But still …' we say.

But still, we're trying desperately to keep the romance alive between ourselves and the mothers of our sons. In between all the arguments about money and the future and our differing parenting styles and worldviews.

When we can afford it we take the mothers of our sons away for romantic weekend city breaks to try to recapture the magic, and we spend the whole time talking about our sons.

We talk about our sons in boutique hotels and restaurants and on the steps of famous tourist attractions. We talk about them while taking in the beautiful views and standing in front of priceless works of art. We reconstruct our entire relationship, again and again, in relation to our sons.

On the steps of the famous tourist attractions we try to remember what it was that first attracted us to each other. In front of the priceless works of art we worry about how much of our relationship is based on what we've already been through, rather than on a mutual vision of the rest of our lives. In the boutique hotels and restaurants we realise we feel like the survivors of a disaster that we can't move on from, and which nobody who wasn't there could possibly understand.

Which is not to say we're comparing the experience of parenthood to a being in a disaster. Not all of it, certainly.

We rope our sons into helping us stage a series of grand romantic gestures, to try to win back the distant, tired hearts of their mothers.

'But you said –'

'Never mind what we said.'

We put together surprise balloon trips, surprise parties and musical performances, organise surprise art installations and events. We book skywriters and ice sculptors and troupes of acrobats. Our sons dress as waiters and ushers and hand out cocktails and canapés while their mothers watch the fabulous sunsets that we've arranged and enjoy the feeling of the volcanic sand between their toes.

Their mothers who we've seen suffer and glow and hope and lose and grieve, over and over again, in order just to get this far. Their mothers who will never know how much it cost us to import that volcanic sand.

And we try to work out how much longer and how well we can rely on all the things we've been through together to stop us falling apart.

Nostalgia

We're teaching our sons about nostalgia.

What it is. Where it comes from. How it was originally diagnosed as a potentially fatal medical condition among seventeenth-century Swiss mercenaries who were suffering from homesickness while fighting in other countries.

Our sons, we've noticed, are incredibly nostalgic. Although not, as yet, in an apparently unhealthy way. They're nostalgic for things that happened a couple of weeks ago, for stuff we did the other day.

'Remember that time the trolls were going to cook the dwarves in that book we read,' they say. 'Remember when we made up that joke. Remember how our younger brothers once did that funny thing.'

'Yes, we do,' we say. 'It was literally yesterday/last night/ this morning.'

'Those were the days,' our sons say.

And we can't argue with that.

As younger men we were almost crushed by nostalgia. From the age of fourteen to at least our early thirties we were constantly trying to recapture whatever feeling it was that we'd previously had at that particular time of year, the last time we'd smelled that perfume, the day we first heard that piece of music. We were obsessed with the changing of the seasons, with fleeting autumn days and mid-summer evenings that went on for ever, with the love affairs we could have had rather than the ones we did. Our idea of perfect happiness was feeling nostalgic for an experience while it was actually still going on.

We weren't so good at processing things in the immediate present. We always had too many questions. Consequently, we missed out on half the significant events of our lives even while they were happening to us.

But, oh, *afterwards* …

Naturally, we don't want this to happen to our sons. We want them to live, as much as possible, in the here and now.

'Look at this beautiful sunset!' we tell them. 'Listen to this wonderful song! Enjoy this perfect moment! But, you know, don't look for *too* long …'

We take them with us to meet one of our oldest friends, who is now The Most Nostalgic Man in the World. The Most Nostalgic Man in the World can remember every moment we ever spent together, remember everything we did and said.

He lives surrounded by fading diaries and scrap books and ledgers, in a house where it's always a late October afternoon and the lengthening shadows never seem to move across the walls.

He drinks too much.

The Most Nostalgic Man in the World fixes us all a drink and together we reminisce about the old days for a while. We realise that since we've become fathers we've been mostly too busy to feel nostalgic about anything. We realise that we don't miss the old days at all.

Nowadays we fail to live in the moment by worrying about the future instead of the past. We worry constantly about everything that could go wrong, about all the awful things that might happen to our sons or to the mothers of our sons or to us or to the rest of the world, about the possibility that there might be things to worry about that we haven't even thought of yet.

We hope we might briefly manage to get the balance right one day, before our sons escape from us for ever.

Practical Life Skills

We're teaching our sons about practical life skills.

We're teaching them how to shave, how to iron a shirt, how to deal with swarms of wasps and bees. We're teaching them how to wire plugs and change tyres and put up shelves, how to bleed radiators and install washing machines. We're bringing in experts to teach them how to buy suits, how to wear a bow tie, what the seven successful habits of the world's most highly effective people are.

The younger sons complain that they're too young for most of this.

'You're never too young!' we shout enthusiastically, trying to ignore the stings of the bees and wasps.

We line our sons up in the empty car park, our massed ranks of sons, and we time them with stopwatches as they assemble kitchen cabinets and repair leaking taps and strip lawnmower engines. Then we get them to do it faster, to do it blindfold, to do it with one hand tied behind their backs, to do it in rain and snowstorms and high winds.

Our sons don't see the point of any of this, don't see why they need these skills. They already have their own YouTube channels and long-term consumer engagement strategies. They upload films of themselves reviewing Lego sets and action figures and playing computer games and doing stunts in the back garden, and then sell their huge audiences to eager advertisers. They're already planning cross-platform multi-media projects involving books, film series, toy tie-ins and video game franchises.

Dealing with failed do-it-yourself projects and swarms of angry insects plays no part in their glorious future.

Our sons hand us our scripts, ask us to go away and learn our lines, give us a couple of days to practise our routines. Then they film us tripping over chairs and falling off collapsing ladders and walking into closed doors and stumbling through plate-glass windows and being knocked down by cars and accidentally getting set on fire, again and again and again, until they're happy they've got what they need.

And we're proud, as we head off to be treated for our concussions and burns and lacerations, our broken arms and legs, just to have played some small part in their success.

Just to have been of use.

Teenage Girls

We're teaching our sons about teenage girls.

How to understand them. How to be friends with them. How to predict their varied moods and movements.

Our sons are confused by the teenage girls, just like everyone else. Nobody knows what to do with them.

We take our sons to places where we can observe teenage girls in their natural habitat – shopping centres and pop concerts, bus stops and libraries, Olympic and Paralympic events, the high desert and the endless steppes. We attempt to blend in with the crowds or the surroundings, pull our hats down over our eyes or camouflage ourselves as rocks, while our sons take hasty notes.

The teenage girls pay no attention to us or our sons. They're too busy shopping and enjoying each other's company, or having mass brawls over stolen boyfriends, or singing along to/performing number one records, or setting fire to suburban bus shelters, or having their first kiss, or writing award-winning poems, or learning to break horses and hunt with eagles, or winning Olympic and Paralympic medals.

Our sons stare, open-mouthed, at the teenage girls.

'What even are they?' they ask.

'They're the future,' we tell them, 'just like you.'

We ask the teenage girls if they can answer some questions. Our older sons stand in the background looking horrified and frantically pantomiming 'NO!' We don't blame them. Between the ages of thirteen and sixteen we were so nervous around girls our age – even the ones we'd known since primary school – that we couldn't even speak in their presence. And look at us now.

It turns out that the teenage girls are too busy to talk to us at the moment, what with all the shopping and gang fights and hunting with eagles.

We take our sons to meet friends of ours who are the fathers of teenage girls. The fathers of the teenage girls sit on their porches, cradling their shotguns as we come down the street. They're twitchy and tired. Their daughters are out late again.

'That's far enough,' the fathers of teenage girls tell us, as we reach their front yards. They ask us what we want with the teenage girls.

'Our sons would like to ask them some questions,' we say. 'To try to understand their perspective on life, what makes them tick, that sort of thing.'

The fathers of the teenage girls look our sons up and down. Squint their eyes at them. Frown.

'Better they don't,' they say.

'But if we could just –'

The fathers of the teenage girls shake their heads, gesture with their shotguns.

'Move along now.'

We turn to apologise to our sons, to come up with another plan, to suggest we all head home, but most of them have already disappeared into the sprawling darkness.

Into the giant and wonderful possibilities of the teenage summer night.

The Abominable Snowman

We're teaching our sons about the Abominable Snowman.

We're telling them about the giant ape-men that feature in the legends of many cultures across the world. We're explaining to them about the Yeti, the Mi-Goh, the Orang Pendek, the Sasquatch, the wild-man of the forest. We're taking them with us on scientific expeditions to the Himalayas that end in disaster as an unidentified creature picks off the members of our party, one by one.

Something that comes out of the blizzard. Something taller than a man …

Our younger sons love the idea of the Abominable Snowman, of Bigfoot, of the Incredible Hulk. They love the idea of pretty much anyone or anything that smashes stuff up and gets away with it. They have adopted these creatures as avatars of their own rage – at their too-early bedtimes, at the food they don't want to eat, at the gigantic unfairness of the world.

Our sons are magnificent in their rage. Their fury is awe-inspiring. We glory in their wrath in a way we were never allowed to glory in our own.

But, all the same, nobody wants them still to be carrying this amount of anger around by the time they become grown men. And, in the meantime, we can't allow them to keep smashing the house up and blaming it all on mythical beasts.

'Why do you think the Abominable Snowman is still so angry at the world?' we ask our sons, as we hold them in our arms in the middle of the trashed bedroom, again, and try to calm them down.

'Nobody understands him,' our sons say, between anguished sobs. 'Nobody listens. And he's probably cold.'

'What do you think would cheer him up?'

'Maybe being allowed to do whatever he wanted,' our sons say, sniffling. They look up at us. 'Maybe not having to clean his teeth so often?'

We sit on the edge of the bed with our young sons in our laps, tuck their heads under our chins, and together we listen to the howling of the wind – and whatever else is out there, in the night and the snow – until they go to sleep.

We stare down at our sons' troubled brows and consider our options, wonder what other parenting techniques we might be able to adopt, think about how we can set a better example to them.

And then we notice the giant wet footprint, too big to be human, in the middle of the bedroom floor.

Violence

We're teaching our sons about violence.

The uses of it. The consequences of it. The meaning of it.

We're taking our sons to unlicensed boxing matches and wedding party punch-ups and Friday night pub car-park fights. We're getting trapped in the middle of ridiculous showdowns between rival football firms, and caught up in pointless turf wars among small-scale local drug gangs. We're watching out-of-shape men assault each other on buses and in supermarkets and on trains and in morning rush hour traffic queues, for no other reason than that they don't know what else to do.

Somewhere along the way, we realise, there's been a terrible mistake. Possibly a sequence of terrible mistakes, stretching right back to the Stone Age.

Under the rain-dazzled street lights our sons stare, wide eyed, at the magnificent horror of it all.

And all those men being punched and kicked to the

ground, we think, all those men punching and kicking each other to the ground must have fathers too, somewhere.

We wonder how their fathers feel about all this.

We've thought about teaching our sons how to fight. How to box, to wrestle, to do karate. We've considered raising an army of miniature ninjas.

If you could see them, all in their black pyjamas, up before dawn every morning to train in the courtyard, the puffs of their icy breath against the watery purple sky, the endless repetition of the same five or six moves, the perfect choreography, their potential careers as professional wrestlers or cage fighters or international assassins ...

We decided against it.

Our fathers never taught us how to fight. We learned how to understand violence all the same. How to walk into any room and know, within seconds, exactly when and how it was going to kick off, and who was going to do the kicking. How to sense that tiniest shift in volume, or temperature, or body language that comes in advance of the first blow.

We're trying not to teach our sons this skill. We don't want them walking around with this knowledge in their heads. This level of paranoia, suspicion, general distrust of half of humanity.

It's never done us any good.

Even when we saw the blow coming there was never anywhere for us to hide.

Rites of Passage

We're teaching our sons about rites of passage.

We're teaching them about the various ways that young men around the world make the transition to manhood and maturity from their callow youth, about the literal and metaphorical tests that they have to pass.

We're taking our sons to see cow jumping ceremonies and bar mitzvahs, to take part in Jugendweihe and Shinbyu celebrations. We're watching adolescent boys throw themselves off the top of hundred-foot-high poles with vines tied to their ankles, or go out onto the savannah armed only with spears to kill their first lion. We're learning about walkabouts and vision quests and the taking of the Athenian Ephebic oath, about Rumspringa and Keshanta. We're witnessing thirteen- and fourteen- and fifteen-year-olds being slapped with stinging nettles for hours on end, or having poison dripped into their eyes, or wearing gloves stitched with stinging bullet ants, or being ritually cut, pierced, scarred and otherwise damaged.

We're disturbed by how many of the ceremonies involve pain and the possibility of death, by what that still says about us as a gender. We're more comfortable with the ceremonies involving extreme drunkenness and altered states of consciousness – but we wonder what that says about *us*, as individuals.

We all like the idea of a quest.

The trans fathers and sons, having already navigated more challenges on the way to manhood than most of us can imagine, deliver a lecture about the stages of The Hero's Journey. Everyone loves the stuff about The Call to Adventure, about the hero's descent into The Belly of the Beast, about The Road of Trials. There's general agreement that the whole Woman-As-Goddess/Woman-As-Temptress thing is a bit problematic these days. We all have something in our eye when it gets to the part about The Atonement with The Father. By the time we reach The Magic Flight and The Return to the World everyone is on their feet cheering.

So we draw up maps and collect supplies, pack our sons' rucksacks and fashion weapons for them from cardboard and foam and gaffer tape. We write lists of enchanted objects to collect on their journey, of magical beings who might help or hinder them on the way. We give them bus timetables and pre-paid mobile phones, just in case they need to call us.

We wait until our sons' mothers have left for work so we can ring school and tell them our sons are having the day off sick. And then we drive them all to the other side of town, to the other side of the river, to the other side of the forest, to the other side of the mountain, and tell them to get started.

Vikings

We're teaching our sons about Vikings.

The Vikings who have intermittently been raiding our towns and villages, bringing death and destruction and theft of our valuables and livestock and women, ever since the eighth century AD. The Vikings who, although they last tried to invade almost a thousand years ago, back in 1066 (just before the more famous invasion by William the Conqueror's Norman army), could potentially return any day.

We're teaching our sons how to spot the shapes of Viking ships on the horizon, how to work out when to flee and where to go, how to bury their valuables and take to the hills and forests and prepare to fight a low-intensity war in the event of the re-establishment of Danelaw.

'What is it with all these effing Vikings?' the younger sons shout, exasperated, throwing up their arms.

And they've got a point.

We have been accused of being over-cautious, of worrying unduly about things that are unlikely to happen. There are more important things to focus on, we're told, than the likelihood of invasion by a culture that largely died out at the end of the eleventh century.

We're troubled by the possibility that the world we're preparing our sons for has already passed us by.

We stand on the edge of the North Sea and look out across the greenish-grey waves, listen to the screaming of the seagulls. We can't see the appeal of any of it. Why couldn't they just stay at home?

'Fortune and glory,' our sons say. 'The thrill of battle. The promise of an eternity in the halls of Valhalla.'

We tell our sons about the giant underwater landslide that took place off the coast of Norway eight thousand years ago, about the tsunami that sent eighty-foot-high waves across the North Sea and halfway up Scotland. We tell them how the waves drowned a collection of low-lying North Sea islands that were all that remained of the former ice-age land bridge – now known as 'Doggerland' – that connected Britain and mainland Europe.

'It was a Palaeolithic Garden of Eden,' we tell our sons. 'Fishermen have been dragging up spear points and stone tools from there for hundreds of years.'

In truth the happy hunting grounds of Doggerland had been doomed since the end of the last ice age, when rising sea levels started to cut the British mainland off from continental Europe. By the time the giant wave came rushing up the beach, we tell our sons, the island chain that had once been the Doggerland hills was probably largely uninhabited.

We visit the historic forts along the Thames Estuary with our sons. Low cloud sits over the entrance to the English Channel and the North Sea, over the power stations and the closed-down oil refineries and the new Thames Gateway deep-water container port.

Our sons man the decommissioned Second World War artillery pieces that sit atop the walls of one of the forts, facing down the grey estuary and out to sea, and keep a look out for Viking sails on the horizon. They aim the sights of the guns at the giant container ships making their way up the Thames from ports all over the world, from Shanghai and Shenzen and Singapore, on the short run over from Rotterdam.

We wonder how it must have felt to be the last men on that last Doggerland island, watching the tide suddenly go out for the very last time.

The Particular Smell of Hospitals at Three in the Morning

We're teaching our sons about the particular smell of hospitals at three in the morning.

The smell of hospitals at three in the morning, we explain to our sons, is mainly the smell of phenols – and in particular meta-cresol (also known as m-Cresol, or 3-methylphenol). Meta-cresol is an organic compound, with the chemical formula $CH_3C_6H_4(OH)$. It's traditionally extracted from coal tar, and has anti-bacterial properties. You'll recognise it as the smell of hospital floor cleaner, the smell of fresh bandages.

At some point in their lives, we tell our sons, everyone ends up getting to know that smell, ends up associating all sorts of memories with it. Like they end up getting to know the pattern of tiles on the floor of at least one particular hospital corridor from walking it, again and again, waiting for news.

Phenols are also present in peat smoke, which is used to dry the malted barley in the production of certain Scotch whiskies. This is why whiskies from the island of Islay remind many people of the smell of hospitals.

Traditionally, men are supposed to drink whisky to celebrate the birth of a child.

We tell our sons about the nights they were born – how their mothers had laboured for hours, working to some deep, seismic rhythm we knew nothing about; how everything felt huge and elemental and far beyond our control.

'It was like spending a night on a mountain in a thunderstorm,' we tell them. 'It was like being lost at sea.'

'And what was it like the first time you saw us?' our sons ask. 'What did we look like?'

'You looked like shaved monkeys,' we tell our sons. 'You looked like wrinkly little old men. You looked like outraged tortoises. It was horrifying.'

We don't tell them about the other nights, about listening to the noise of machines and watching their mothers' shallow breathing as they slept. About the vast and holy silence that fills a hospital at three in the morning.

We don't tell them about going home alone in the early hours of the morning, again and again, to houses and flats that would not be filled with life and noise. About trying to pick things up and put things back together over the next days and weeks and months.

These are not things we talk about, not even to each other. Especially not to each other.

We're terrified that if we started we wouldn't know how to stop.

The War Against
the Potato Beetle

We're teaching our sons about the war against the potato beetle.

Because it's important to know your history. Because it's important to be prepared.

'In East Germany, in the nineteen-fifties,' we explain, 'the national potato crop of the GDR was severely threatened by the spread of Colorado beetles. Because the larvae of the beetle fed exclusively on the leaves of the potato plant and had few natural predators, the beetle had the potential to wipe out up to one hundred per cent of one of the country's staple foods.

'To counter this threat to the Deutsche Demokratische Republik,' we continue, 'East German school children were tasked with collecting as many Colorado beetle larvae as they could find. They were told that the beetles had been dropped from imperialist American planes in an attempt to destabilise the East German economy. Children who collected particularly large numbers of beetle larvae were celebrated as national heroes.'

'How big were the beetles?' our sons ask.

'You know, beetle-sized,' we say.

Our sons are disappointed. They'd imagined it as a war against giant beetles. Maybe just one single beetle that was bigger than a row of houses, bigger than a tractor factory. A beetle that could have singlehandedly (multi-footedly?) destroyed the fledgling East German people's republic, had it not been stopped by brave school kids armed with flame-throwers and bazookas.

'No, it wasn't like that,' we say.

A single, giant beetle, parachuting down over Potsdam from an American B-25 bomber. A giant, radioactive beetle which had been accidentally – or maybe not so accidentally – created as a result of atomic testing in the Nevada desert.

The ultimate weapon.

'No.'

'Did any of this even actually happen?' our sons ask, disappointed.

And we wonder: did it?

We have memories of the Colorado beetle threat being discussed by our parents when we were children – but this was in the UK in the nineteen-eighties, not East Germany in the fifties. We remember a summer spent keeping our eyes open for the tiny, striped invaders, remember running to our parents to show them whenever we spotted something likely, but the memory is mixed up with that of an invasion of biting ladybirds that surely happened at another time.

'Ladybirds can bite you?' our sons ask, horrified.

'It's just a nip, really, you wouldn't –'

'Are they as poisonous as Brazilian wandering spiders? Would you die?'

'No, you wouldn't die.'

They narrow their eyes, unconvinced.

We don't blame them.

We remember the afternoon the swarm descended on the playground, and the children cowering under desks or running screaming from the school gates, the muffled screams of children staggering from classrooms covered in millions of red and black biting insects.

The eyes.

They eat your eyes first.

Relativity

We're teaching our sons about relativity.

We're teaching them about velocity and distance and time, about how the speed of light in a vacuum is the same everywhere in the universe, about how clocks run at different rates on earth and on the International Space Station. We're setting up demonstrations of the fundamental principles with tennis balls and moving vehicles and observations of the transit of the planet Venus across the sun during solar eclipses.

'Imagine you are a photon, travelling close to the event horizon of a black hole,' we say to our sons. 'Imagine you were on a spaceship, moving almost at the speed of light.'

We scrawl the equations on giant blackboards and all over the walls and windows of our sons' bedrooms, just like we've seen scientists do on television.

'Imagine coming back to earth after five years in space and discovering that your younger brothers are now older than you,' we say.

The younger sons are delighted by this. They consider the reign of terror they could embark upon; the horrible revenge they could visit on their older brothers for the years of unfairness they've had to endure.

'What would happen if you were on a bus going at fifty miles an hour and you shot a gun at someone on another bus that was driving towards you at a hundred miles an hour?' the younger sons ask. 'Would it still kill them?'

'Nobody is killing anyone,' say the mothers of our sons, 'we've discussed this.'

And, of course, they're right.

We try, ourselves and the mothers of our sons, to present a united front as much as is possible. We know how quickly things could go wrong if our sons were able to exploit any differences between us. Sensible bedtimes and a healthy diet would go out of the window within hours. The house would be destroyed before the end of the week.

And yet we can feel ourselves moving apart, like wandering moons being pulled into eccentric new orbits around the gigantic fact of our children – sometimes in opposition to each other, occasionally passing close enough to wave and shout a hello, always hoping that our relative trajectories don't end up intersecting catastrophically.

Pirates

We're teaching our sons about pirates.

Our sons, of course, love the idea of pirates, want to know everything about them. Because pirates get to wear great outfits and have cutlass fights, they tell us. Because pirates get to do whatever they want.

We try to explain the reality of the international shipping business, about standardised intermodal containerisation, and deep-water ports, and the just-in-time global economy. About speedboats full of desperate, unemployed Somalian fishermen armed with RPGs. About the realities of the ransom business and maritime law and marine insurance.

'But real pirates aren't … they're not –'

Our sons don't want to listen. They want romance and adventure and life on the high seas. Just like everybody else.

We rent rowing boats and take our sons on a canal trip. It's early in the morning and mist drifts across the surface of the water. The canals are full of shopping trolleys and dead foxes and ferocious, non-native terrapins. The terrapins glide through the weeds and snap at our fingers, occasionally drag ducks and geese under the water. Our sons, dressed in orange life jackets, are unimpressed.

We keep expecting to come across a dead body, bloated and white, picked apart by terrapins and invasive North American crayfish.

We tie up the boats alongside an abandoned factory and distribute the packed lunches. There are chocolate coins wrapped in gold and silver foil, but nobody is fooled. Railway bridges and the unloved backs of warehouses loom over us. We don't even recognise where we are any more.

Somewhere in the distance we can hear the sounds of an all-night rave still going on.

It's starting to look like rain.

And then, from under the railway bridge, suddenly bearing down on us, the ship appears out of the mist.

The figurehead at the bow is a shop-window dummy sprayed silver and wearing a gas mask. It holds aloft an anarchist flag. The hull is painted with rainbows and skulls and leaping dolphins, and a couple of mangy dogs lean over the side, barking in our direction. From the wheelhouse a giant skull and crossbones flag snaps in the wind. And on the deck the ragged crew of young men and women are dancing, oblivious, to the booming music.

We all watch, stunned, as the ghostly ship cruises past. Our tiny boats lift and bump on the swell.

'You see?' our sons shout, in triumph. 'You see?'

Hotels

We're teaching our sons about hotels.

We're taking them on business trips and showing them how to get free upgrades and how to tip room service and what to steal on your way out, how not to look like you shouldn't be there.

We don't know if we've ever managed to successfully not look like we shouldn't be there. We've certainly never managed to successfully not *feel* like we shouldn't be there.

Our sons like the breakfasts best. They can't believe that all the food is free, or that you can have cake for breakfast.

'Well, technically it's not free,' we say. 'Somebody's paying. Someone is always paying, somewhere.'

In the hotel bars in the evenings everyone tries to line up extramarital affairs and one-night stands. Everyone except us and our sons.

We consider the possibilities of being unfaithful to the mothers of our sons, try to work out if having some sort of fling is right for us. We go over the potential benefits, the logistics involved, the consequences.

We identify a number of issues, including:

- We have no idea who to be unfaithful to the mothers of our sons with.
- We already have enough things to worry about.
- We're not sure what the problem we're trying to solve actually *is*.

There's the danger of getting caught to take into account, too – the chance of losing everything. Not to mention our general love and respect for the mothers of our sons. We don't want to hurt them unnecessarily or put them in uncomfortable situations.

'These sorts of things are not to be entered into lightly,' the divorced and separated fathers agree. The divorced and separated fathers are trying especially hard to line up one-night stands in the hotel bar. We're not judging them.

We think about the kinds of people who we might like to have some sort of clandestine relationship with, try to work out if they're the same kind of people who might be interested in having a clandestine relationship with us.

We realise that we hardly know anyone these days.

We wonder if the mothers of our sons are having secret love affairs, or have already had them, or are planning to at some point in the future. We're not taking anything for granted. We've seen the way the divorced and separated fathers look at the mothers of our sons. We know how it goes. The divorced and separated fathers assure us that the mothers of our sons are not having secret love affairs with them. But then, we'd say the same thing, in their position.

Do we even want to have affairs, we wonder, or do we just want to be someone else for a while? To be seen through someone else's eyes?

'What are you all talking about?' our sons ask. They've finished the complimentary bar snacks, are getting bored. We realise that hotel bars are no places for children. Or for fathers.

So we take our sons upstairs to watch cartoons in our rooms and raid the mini bars, while we work out what else we can get away with stealing.

The Aftermath of Disasters

We're teaching our sons about the aftermath of disasters.

We're helping them understand the moments when the dust has started to settle and the debris has been cleared away and everyone comes together to try to work out what just happened, what it means to them. We're helping them negotiate the public outpourings of grief, the candlelit vigils, the blood donations, the fundraising memorial concerts, the announcement of the parliamentary inquiry.

We've agreed in advance with the mothers of our sons how we'll talk about these things, how we'll deal with any questions our sons have. It's becoming a habit. But we have no real answers to why people keep dying in fires and train crashes and terrorist atrocities, why they keep dying in earthquakes and floods and industrial accidents. None that help, anyway.

We want our sons to feel empathy, to be involved in humanity, but this is too much.

We take our sons to attend the vigils, observe the two-minute silences with them. They're experts at this, by now. At their schools they're already collecting stuff and trying to raise money to help. Every day they go to school wearing clothes in a different colour for a different cause.

'The thing about disasters,' we tell our sons, because this is what we've been told to say, 'is that you should focus on the way everyone helps each other afterwards. Doctors and nurses and firefighters and members of the public and so on.'

Our sons nod, having heard this countless times before. They're much better adjusted to the experience than we are. They have a fine sense of slapstick, of the absurd. They understand the world perfectly well in terms of buildings collapsing around people's ears, of people getting hit with frying pans and falling objects, of people falling down flights of stairs, of cars that fall apart when you put the key in the ignition, of things falling out of the sky.

And we still have to keep letting them go out in the world. We have to keep pretending that we aren't terrified – like cartoon characters who've run off a cliff, their legs still going, convincing themselves not to look down.

We try to remember how we got through the aftermath of each of our catastrophes, each of our shared disasters, and we can't recall ever even discussing them with anyone.

Because what was there that anyone could say?

All we remember is being unable to understand how everyone was still getting on with their lives, still walking around in the world, while we stood frozen to the spot, waiting for the arrival of the falling grand piano that would finally make sense of everything.

Drinking

We're teaching our sons about drinking.

We're teaching them about vintage wine and artisanal beer and hand-crafted spirits. We're taking them with us to wine tastings and on whisky tours. We're looking forward to the days when we'll get drunk with our sons, when we'll have competitions to see who can drink who under the table.

Their mothers, of course, don't approve. Their wonderful mothers, who, for the purposes of this part of the story, we're casting in the role of the bad cop, the sensible parent, the straight man. Their wonderful mothers who deserve better than this.

We're taking our sons to all the places we've ever been drunk, to the sites of some of our finest hours. We're taking them to pubs and cocktail bars and airport lounges and squats and friends' bedrooms and sublet council flats belonging to friends of our parents and multi-storey car parks with fantastic views and a seaside town in Mexico where we once spent a week holed up with a case of Kahlua.

Kahlua, for goodness' sake.

We take them to the pub where we once spent an entire day drinking, eleven in the morning through to eleven at night, just to see if we could. It was years ago. Nobody there remembers us now. We're not even sure if it was the same pub.

We take them to the bridge over the ring road where, as much younger men, we once had a spectacular kiss against a washed-out dawn sky with a beautiful woman who we were trying to convince to run away with us.

'That was the booze talking,' we explain.

Our sons don't get it.

'But what was the point of it all?' they ask.

We don't take our sons to the place under another bridge where we used to drink bottles of cider with aspirins crumbled into them when we were thirteen. There are limits.

The divorced and separated and widowed dads take us all to the bars and nightclubs where they still go, against desperate odds, in the hope of meeting eligible women. The divorced and separated and widowed dads line up along the bar, trying to look nonchalant and thin. Trying to look five or ten or fifteen years younger.

Our sons try not to cramp their style.

'Most of the time,' we say, 'it was just an excuse to stay up all night.'

Our sons get that. They hate going to bed.

These days we fall asleep before they do.

And then we get up before dawn, check all the doors and windows, and sit at the kitchen table for hours, waiting quietly in the half-light for the arrival of one more bright and possible day.

The Pointlessness of Guilt

We're teaching our sons about the pointlessness of guilt.

That is, we've been trying to teach our sons about the pointlessness of guilt, but we're at a soft play centre for a birthday party, so no one's paying much attention.

The soft play centre is terrifying. The children have all had about three kilograms of sugar and they're playing on thirty-foot-high scaffolding with some foam taped to it. Sooner or later, everyone inside the soft play centre knows, there's going to be a horrible accident.

We try to take our minds off the impending horror by flirting with the other children's mothers. It's no good. We don't know how to flirt, and the mothers have better things to worry about. Flirting with middle-aged fathers is the last thing they need. What they need is more coffee.

The children are jumping onto each other from the summit of the thirty-foot-high scaffolding now. Each one of them looks like a potential murderer. Each one of them except our beautiful sons.

'Do you think someone should –' we start to say, but the mothers have already wandered off to find coffee, leaving us to wrestle with our terror and our pointless guilt.

We feel guilty about falling down the stairs while carrying our sons when they were six months old, causing them to break their left legs. They were only in plaster for two weeks, but when they didn't walk until they were fifteen months old we were convinced that we'd damaged them permanently. We still wonder if they'll curse our names on cold, damp winter days long after we're gone.

We feel guilty about our fear of everything, and about not having a sunnier outlook on life, and about not having enough time to spend with our sons, and about not always wanting to have enough time to spend with our sons.

We feel guilty about the lousy genetic legacies we've handed on to our sons, which may predispose them to – among other things – high blood pressure, or colour blindness, or sickle cell anaemia, or short-sightedness, or depression and other mental illnesses, or heart disease, or alcoholism, or drug addiction, or diabetes, or Tay-Sachs disease, or autistic spectrum disorders, or obesity, or suicide, or certain types of cancer, or arthritis, or worse.

We feel guilty about the environment that our sons are

growing up in (chiefly: *being our sons*), which may also predis-
pose them to many of the above.

We feel guilty about flirting (about attempting to flirt)
with the distracted mothers at the soft play centre who have
far better things to worry about.

And, of course, we feel guilty knowing that our guilt
about all these things doesn't help. And neither does feeling
guilty about our guilt, and so on, and so on, and so on.

When one of our sons finally falls from the scaffolding
and cuts his head open and we're called upon to make
everything better it's actually a relief.

War

We're teaching our sons about war.

We're taking them on coach trips to visit famous First World War battlefields, on visits to museums full of tanks and cannons, on days out to look at the remains of Second World War defences along the English and French coasts.

We gaze in wonder at the crumbling giant bunkers and concrete listening dishes that face each other across the Channel, eat our sandwiches while watching middle-aged men perform reconstructions of scenes from the Wars of the Roses.

Now there's a thing to do for a living, we think.

Our sons, of course, love the idea of war. The chaos. The weapons. The disruption of the everyday order of things. The abandoned tea time and bath time and bed time rules.

Not to mention all the technological and social developments that war inspires.

'War,' our younger sons remind us, 'is the locomotive of history, after all.'

Then they stare, pointedly, at their older brothers, just long enough to make them start getting nervous again.

Together with our sons we stand on the edge of the continent watching the evening skies roll in. We try to imagine the ranks of aircraft taking off behind us on their way to flatten half of Europe, the ranks of aircraft coming the other way to rain high-explosive history down on our sons. We explain to our sons why there are fifteen houses missing from our street, why there's a school built in the middle of a terrace. We tell them about Anderson shelters and Morrison shelters and V1s and V2s. About evacuees.

We try to ask ourselves what we would do, what we would have done, given the choice. Whether we could send our sons away or keep them with us to take their chances, if it came to that.

There's no good answer.

But that night we lie down next to our sons while they sleep, wrap our arms around their thin chests, put our faces into their hair. And we know, selfishly, that we would have chosen to go like this, holding on to our sons, rather than risk letting them slip away to face the world alone, and never getting to say goodbye.

And we are not proud of that.

The Fifteen Foolproof Approaches to Making Someone Fall in Love with You

We're teaching our sons about the fifteen foolproof approaches to making someone fall in love with you.

We're teaching our sons this for free, even though there are, apparently, men who make money teaching this kind of thing to other men, and entire conferences and online courses and businesses built on the back of it.

We don't know if there are any women who make money teaching this kind of thing to men, although that would surely make more sense in a lot of cases.

We walk our sons through each of the fifteen foolproof approaches to making someone fall in love with you. The approaches include handsomeness, charm, decency, kindness to animals, humour, being passionate about things, romance, and sexual magnetism.

We explain that sexual magnetism is not the same as actual magnetism, which is what our sons have been learning about at school. We've spent most of the weekend testing every object and every surface in the house for their magnetic properties. The weekend before it was designing shields for Roman soldiers.

We tell our sons about the early days of our relationships with their mothers, explain which of the fifteen foolproof approaches worked on roughly thirty-seven per cent of them, which were unsuccessful sixty-five per cent of the time, and so on. According to the numbers, sexual magnetism actually turns out to have been a successful opener for almost twenty per cent of our sons' mothers.

'Ha!' say our sons' mothers.

'What?' we ask.

'Nothing,' say our sons' mothers. 'Please, carry on. Pretend we're not here.'

'The most important thing to remember,' we tell our sons, 'is that love is a verb, not a noun. Love isn't a thing. Love is something you do.'

We're not sure where we got that from, although it sounds true.

We look across at our sons' mothers, are filled all over again with respect and admiration for them, are simultaneously irritated by things like the way they leave letters and keys and lip salve in a pile in front of the drawer where all the takeaway menus are, so that we have to shift everything out of the way every time we want to open the drawer.

We don't share this with our sons.

The divorced and separated and widowed fathers, with their own perspective on things, look out of the window at the gigantic spring skies and plan their next moves.

Life

We're teaching our sons about life.

What it's all about, how it works, the origins of it.

We're in what looks suspiciously like a mad scientist's laboratory from a nineteen-thirties horror film. There are banks of dials and switches everywhere, and electricity arcs and leaps between huge metal coils. In the centre of the room a giant, sheet-covered body on a table is being winched up towards the open roof, where lightning forks across the sky.

Our sons are all wearing goggles and miniature lab coats. They look adorable. They pull levers and throw switches while the divorced and separated and widowed fathers take it in turns to chat up the local peasant girls who are moonlighting as our glamorous assistants.

'Life on earth evolved around four and a half billion years ago,' we explain. 'Initially, life was –'

'What about rocks?' our sons ask.

'What?'

'Are rocks alive?'

'No,' we say, 'rocks aren't alive. Pull that lever. No, the one on the left. No, the other left.'

Our sons do as we ask. The crashing of thunder fills the laboratory. On the table, high above us now, the creature's dead hand slips from under the sheet, twitching.

'What about lava?' our sons ask.

'Lava is just melted rock.'

'Can anything destroy lava?'

'No, it –'

'When lava hits water it cools down and turns back into rock,' the older sons say.

'Yes, that's exactly what happens.'

'But lava was around before rocks were?'

'Well, it would be a combination of – can you wind those handles now? – a combination of rocks and lava.'

'Where did water come from?'

'Comets,' we say, 'the water probably came from comets. But, look, this was all long before –'

'How can electricity make things come back to life anyway?' our sons ask, as the table reaches the top of the winch with a jolt.

It's taken us six months to find the creature, frozen in the ice in the collapsed catacombs under the burnt-down windmill. Another two months to get it out. The locals were suspicious – there were bribes and permits to take care of, daughters to be declared off-limits to the attentions of the divorced and separated and widowed fathers.

But now we're moments away from the culmination of a lifetime's work.

High on the table the creature's body arches as the lightning flows through it. We think about our Nobel prize speech, what we'll do with all the money and the fame.

The life we'll be able to build for our sons.

Then the pitchfork-wielding locals – who have come to snatch their daughters back from the divorced and separated and widowed fathers – break down the door and set fire to everything with their flaming torches.

Later, in the airport as we wait for our flight to be called, our sons bring us copies of the local paper, show us the story about the sightings of the creature. They know how badly we're taking this.

They put their arms around our shoulders.

'Tell us how life first evolved,' they say, kindly. 'Tell us again.'

The Wonderful Colours of the Non-Neurotypical Spectrum

We're teaching our sons about the wonderful colours of the non-neurotypical spectrum.

We're teaching them about what the spectrum is, and what it means, and where some of them and some of us might be on it. We're teaching them about how a person's position on the spectrum might manifest itself in the particular things that they're interested in, and/or how they might behave.

'It's a spectrum,' we explain, 'lots of people are on it. That's the point of it.'

Some of us, of course, are more on it than others. Statistically, that is. The spectrum is nothing if not a broad church.

We're currently in a branch of Games Workshop, about to buy our sons their first set of miniature role-playing figures. As we were once taken by our fathers to buy our own first set.

Our sons stare in wonder at the rows and rows of tiny plastic orcs and space marines, at the shelves full of rule books, at the trays full of four-sided and six-sided and eight-sided and ten-sided and twelve-sided and twenty-sided dice.

Nowadays, we explain to our sons, you can't move for all the non-neurotypical people in films and books and television series. And of course they're all geniuses and superheroes. But where were they when we were growing up?

Where were they when we were playing Dungeons and Dragons and writing computer programs in our bedrooms and wondering why we were so weird? Who did *those fathers among us who are on the spectrum* have to identify with?

Not, as we remind our sons, that this is about us. This is about our sons, wherever they are, on and off the spectrum.

Our wonderful sons, who talk too loud or who don't talk at all. Our wonderful sons who don't always understand that other people might not share their enthusiasms. Our sometimes withdrawn and distant wonderful sons. Our wonderful sons who absolutely cannot keep still. Our wonderful sons who go to places where we can't follow. Our wonderful sons who were obsessed with jigsaw puzzles at the age of two. Our wonderful sons who may or may not struggle with eye contact. Our wonderful sons who are statistically more likely to be interested in Dungeons and Dragons and other role-playing games, but only statistically. Our wonderful, systematising sons. Our wonderful sons who might find it difficult to interpret non-verbal social cues. Our wonderful, often overly literal sons. Our wonderful sons who may or may not struggle to know what is and isn't appropriate in polite conversation. Our wonderful sons who sometimes can't cope with loud noises, or certain textures against their skins. Our wonderful sons who like to do things a certain way, who always eat their dinner, for instance, one type of food at a time. Our wonderful sons who can't do small talk. Our wonderful list-making sons.

Our wonderful, beautiful, hilarious sons.

Martians

We're teaching our sons about Martians.

For the last few weeks a group of lonely billionaires have been all over the news talking about their plans to populate the Red Planet. They're auditioning for brave and clever and able-bodied young men and women to help them build dynamic new low-tax civilisations on Mars and across the asteroid belt.

In return they're promising adventure and excitement and the potential for heroic deaths.

Naturally, our sons are intrigued. For as long as they can remember they've been following the adventures of the unmanned *Curiosity* and *Opportunity* rovers as they roam the planet's dusty surface. Those brave robots seem almost like family members.

'Can we go to Mars?' our sons ask us.

We're not unsympathetic. When we were children our fathers read *The War of the Worlds* to us as a bedtime story. We remember glorying in the destruction of Woking and London, which seemed like far less interesting places than the Martian invaders' home planet. When we were our sons' age we wanted to go to Mars too.

It's the potential for heroic deaths bit that we're not comfortable with.

'What about the radiation?' we ask. 'Without the protection of the earth's magnetic field you're going to be exposed to constant bombardment from cosmic rays.'

'We're young,' our sons say, 'what does radiation matter to us? We're indestructible.'

'Space sickness,' we say. 'Explosive decompression. Muscle atrophy and shrinking spines caused by low gravity. And that's just the journey there. Do you know how many Mars missions have crashed on landing?'

'It's the guy who invented battery-powered sports cars,' our sons insist. 'If he doesn't know how to successfully land spaceships, who does?'

'What about aliens?' we ask. 'Or deadly space bacteria? Or meteorites? Or dust storms?'

Our sons look at us.

'You can't protect us from the everyday dangers of life in the solar system,' our sons say. 'Sooner or later you're going to have to let us go break our hearts on the sharp edges of the universe, whether you like it or not.'

So we tell them we'll think about it.

It's the fifth of August. We realise that somewhere on Mars the plucky little *Curiosity* rover will be playing 'Happy Birthday' to itself, as it has been programmed to do on the same day every year since its touchdown in 2012.

We imagine our brave sons topping some Martian hill, watching as the pale and distant sun rises on their cold and beautiful new world, forty million miles away from our arms.

We wonder what songs they'll sing.

The Ones that Got Away

We're teaching our sons about the ones that got away.

We're teaching them about missed opportunities, and roads not taken, and bad timing, and bad luck. We're explaining how every choice that a person makes, or doesn't make, ends up contributing to the way that their life turns out. We're telling them that sometimes it doesn't matter what choices you arrive at, or how well you plan, or how hard you want or deserve something.

'Sometimes the odds are just against you,' we say, and sigh for emphasis.

'So you just think about that next time,' the younger sons tell their older brothers, narrowing their eyes and drawing their fingers across their throats.

We take our sons on a tour of all the places where we've made spectacularly bad decisions, where we couldn't talk our way out of things any more, where we ran out of luck. Where the courses of our lives took huge and irreversible turns, whether we liked it or not.

We have to hire a fleet of buses to accommodate everyone, book the hotels in advance.

We visit out-of-season Dutch seaside towns and French vineyards and Finnish saunas and the Baikonur Cosmodrome in southern Kazakhstan. We go back to beach parties in south-east Asia that have been running, non-stop, for over twenty years. We stand on the decks of wrecked oil tankers and wish we could have shouted 'port' instead of 'starboard'. We stare up at the big walls of Yosemite and remember the knots that didn't hold.

We think about the ones who got away, wondering where many of them are now.

In fact, we know exactly where many of them are now. We looked on the internet. It took us about five minutes. They're happily married or single or cohabiting or living in experimental modern partnerships, with or without children or their dream careers or challenging situations to overcome. With exactly the same big and small problems as everyone else.

'Does everyone always end up wishing their lives had turned out differently?' our sons ask. They've been thinking things over. We've all been on the bus for hours, driving through endless banana plantations. We're not sure what country we're in, or why we're here.

'We don't wish our lives had turned out differently,' we say, turning to our sons, and we mean it. 'If our lives had turned out differently then we wouldn't have had you.'

'You might have had other children though.'

'They wouldn't have been as good as you.'

'Everyone says that about their children.'

'That's because it's true,' we say.

And it is.

Our sons digest what we've been saying. We think about the children we didn't have, remember what that felt like, remember what we would have given, then, for things to be different.

'You might have had girls,' our sons say, with mock horror.

'Girls are all right,' we say. 'Your cousins are girls. They're great.'

'Still.'

We think about it.

'Yeah, it would be weird, wouldn't it?'

Our sons put their heads on our shoulders, watch the banana trees going by out of the bus window. And we know that, given the choice, we would be happy to lose everything again, and more, just to end up here – wherever here even is – right at this moment.

Right now.

Video Games

We're teaching our sons about video games.

We're telling them how video games have helped get us through some of the most difficult times in our lives, and how they've made us miss out on some other times altogether. We're explaining how video games cemented our most important relationships, and how they were responsible for the loss of at least half of our twenties. And our thirties.

We tell them how their mothers spent hours playing Tomb Raider and Prince of Persia when they were pregnant, sitting on giant bean bags in front of the TV.

We don't tell them about how, as thirteen-year-olds, we sneaked out of school to play Dragon's Lair in the arcade in town the day it was released. Even our own fathers don't know that. We don't want to be giving our sons any ideas.

'You're standing too close to the screen,' we keep telling our sons.

Our sons wait until we leave the room again, and then all shuffle back to where they were before.

We tell our sons the story of the boy whose father died when he was very young, leaving him with scattered memories of their time spent playing video games together – and an old games console that the boy couldn't bear to look at for ten years.

When the boy finally turned the machine back on at the age of sixteen, we tell our sons, he found that his father's best lap from the racing game they used to play together was still saved on the hard drive.

His father, preserved for ever as the ghost car you race against when you're trying to improve your lap time.

His father, endlessly speeding away from him, as the boy spent the next few months playing the game obsessively, gaining a few fractions of a second every day.

Imagining his father's hands on the wheel of the car in front, his father's eyes in the mirror.

Until the day that the boy became good enough that he was able to catch and overtake his father's car, and watch him recede into the distance. And then be wiped from the machine's memory as the boy crossed the finish line, his own perfect lap finally replacing the old man's.

Our sons glance at us, look back to the screen.

'But how does that even –'

We sit down next to them, pick up the spare controller.

We've got a few years on them yet.

The Extinction of the Dinosaurs

We're teaching our sons about the extinction of the dinosaurs.

As all fathers, everywhere, must eventually teach their sons.

We're teaching them about the impact of the fifteen-kilometre-wide asteroid or comet that struck the shallow seas off the coast of Mexico approximately sixty-six million years ago, and which likely threw so much rock into the atmosphere that the sun was blocked out for a year. We're explaining about the short-term effects of the global firestorm and the long-term effects of the global winter that followed the impact.

'Everything that didn't burn to death, starved,' we tell our sons. 'Pterosaurs and dinosaurs on land. Plesiosaurs and mosasaurs and ammonites in the sea. Just about every animal on earth that weighed more than around twenty-five kilograms went extinct.'

'Except crocodiles,' our sons say. 'Crocodiles survived.'

'Well, yes, except crocodiles,' we say. 'But crocodiles can go without food for a very long time.'

'But if crocodiles could survive ...' our sons say, 'then how can we be sure about everything else?'

'Crocodiles are ectothermic!' we say. 'Plus, they live in streams. Animals that live in streams tend to feed on detritus that gets washed in from the land. There were dead animals everywhere. That's a very specific, specialist food source. Most animals couldn't have exploited that niche.'

Our sons just look at us. They've heard this argument before.

So we put together a series of expeditions to explore the Venezuelan jungle, the remote mountains of New Guinea, the high Antarctic desert. We send mini-subs to the bottom of the Atlantic and Pacific oceans. We spend two years contracting horrible tropical diseases, and accidentally discovering new species of man-eating snakes and giant spiders, and rewriting the history of the last ice age.

But no dinosaurs.

Our sons remain unconvinced.

'Dragons, too,' they say.

There follows a stand-off. Until eventually, inevitably, we give up.

'Okay, fine,' we say, admitting defeat. 'Dinosaurs and dragons still exist. Somewhere.'

Our sons are satisfied with that. Everyone goes away happy.

But.

But one day, we promise ourselves, we'll explain to them that the asteroid-induced catastrophe at the end of the Cretaceous period was only one of at least five generally recognised global extinctions – and that it wasn't even the largest.

The Permian-Triassic extinction 250 million years ago, we'll tell them, killed more than seventy per cent of all land animals on the planet, and over ninety-five per cent of all marine life. Even insects.

That'll give them something to think about, we decide. That'll give them pause.

Art

We're teaching our sons about art.

We're teaching them how to look at art, how to think about it, how to ask questions about what it is and what it isn't. We're explaining to them about painting and sculpture and print making and conceptual art and performance art, with practical demonstrations.

We take them to an art gallery where a heroic artist is putting on a piece of performance art. We've checked in advance that the performance is suitable for minors. Because you never know.

It turns out that the gallery is full of parents and children. It's half term and everyone is desperate for something to do, something to look at, some excuse to get out of the house. And art is as good as any other temporary distraction.

In the middle of the art gallery the heroic artist sits in a cage wearing running shorts. The heroic artist has a huge artistic beard. The programme tells us that the heroic artist has been inside the cage for a week now. For the past week, inside the cage, the heroic artist has been getting on with the ordinary business of his life, which consists of thinking artistic thoughts, eating, sleeping, appearing in magazines and on television and on websites, and going to the toilet.

To accommodate all this there are a table, a chair, a bed, a phone, a laptop and a portaloo inside the cage.

It's quite a big cage.

We watch the heroic artist going about his business for a while. Nothing much happens. We wonder if that's supposed to be the point.

'What do you think about the piece?' we ask our sons, as we all stand around stroking our chins. 'What does it mean?'

The heroic artist looks up. He's interested to know what our sons think too. He's wondering if he'll be able to incorporate their thoughts and opinions into his show, to widen his appeal.

'Maybe it would be better if there were wild animals in there with him?' our sons say. 'And the artist only had a certain amount of time to escape from the cage. To make things more interesting for everyone. Not for the man to die. Not necessarily.'

We raise our eyebrows at the artist.

He stares back at us, not sure what he should do next.

Women, Again

We're teaching our sons about women, again.

As if the last time wasn't bad enough.

Our sons give us a list of all the important things that we've failed to cover so far. It includes male–female friendships, the experience of having sisters, women in the workplace, female superheroes, violence against women, famous women throughout history, the tallest woman who ever lived, feminine archetypes in literature and film, consent, discrimination, The Ten Most Dangerous Women in the World, equal pay, and the woefully inadequate provision for women's sexual and reproductive health around the world, including in otherwise 'developed' countries.

'Among other issues,' our sons say.

'Of course,' we say.

We are not unaware of the importance of getting this right. For everyone's sake. We take the responsibility of raising a generation of better men, of better people, seriously. So we ask our sons to give us time to pull together some sort of presentation for them, to do some more research.

They agree to give us a month.

'Women ninjas,' say the younger sons. 'Include some women ninjas.'

'Women ninjas. Right.'

'And a lady dragon.'

'Okay.'

We are aware that our attitudes to women are a work in progress. We've had to re-evaluate our opinions and past behaviour a number of times, usually following exposés of the activities of rich and powerful men. We've had to ask ourselves 'Is this us? Is that who we are? Are these the men we want our sons to be?'

And this, of course, is a good thing. There's a lot to be undone. We're taking nothing for granted. We don't want our sons to be defined by their gender any more than we want women to be defined by theirs. Any more than we want to be defined by ours.

We don't mind being defined by our roles as fathers, all things considered.

We know we've had a tendency to romanticise women in the past, to idealise them as mythical beings with special powers, to imagine they could grant us life-changing wishes if we could only win their hearts by completing a series of impossible, fantastical tasks. Thankfully, parenthood knocked most of that right out of us.

But we're also up against the clock.

And so we spend the next two weeks searching uncharted seas and cutting our way through an impenetrable jungle before free climbing an unmapped escarpment and fighting our way across a haunted cloud forest to the fabulous ice cave where The World's Most Beautiful Women guard the secret archive that contains all the answers.

They've been expecting us.

And it's clear from the look on their faces that we're not off the hook yet.

The Importance of Good Posture and Looking After your Teeth

We're teaching our sons about the importance of good posture and looking after your teeth.

We're teaching them about the dangers of plaque and tooth decay and gingivitis, about the potential debilitating effects of chronic back pain in later life. We're reminding them about getting regular exercise and drinking lots of water. We're warning them not to stand too close to the television, or the microwave, or our mobile phones.

The mundanity of it all is crushing, we know. But we've invested a lot in our sons' fragile bodies, we tell them. We want them to look after those bodies for as long as they can.

'Look at us,' we say to our sons. 'We're falling apart.'

'We know,' our sons tell us, without even looking up.

We tell our sons, again, about the times when we broke our ankles, and our wrists, and our ribs, and our collar bones, about our torn knee ligaments and exploded Achilles tendons and collapsed discs, about our failing eyes and ears and prostates.

'It's not the age,' we tell our sons proudly, 'it's the mileage.'

We attempt to compare injuries with our sons' mothers. The mothers look at us, amused.

'Are you kidding?' they say.

By the time we realise our mistake it's already too late.

The mothers order bottles of white wine, start discussing the impositions and indignities visited on their bodies by multiple pregnancies and childbirth and breastfeeding. They share horror stories of tears and stitches and weakened pelvic floors and blocked milk ducts and much, much worse. They explain why they can never go on a trampoline again.

It's nightmarish. We don't want our sons to hear this. We don't even want to hear this ourselves, and we were there when most of it happened.

We throw ourselves on the mercy of our sons' mothers, beg their forgiveness. We promise to worship and respect their bodies for ever, in whatever state of sexy decline they happen to be. It's the least we can do. Frankly, we're amazed that they can look at any of us without wanting to kill us.

'Most of the time,' they say. 'Only most of the time.'

We bathe our sons and brush their hair, inspect their skin and look in their eyes. We check between their toes, and count their teeth again. We scrub under their nails.

They indulge us, patiently.

Then they go back to climbing walls and falling off bikes and skateboards and throwing themselves out of windows and off the roofs of houses, with no consideration or thought for the future whatsoever.

Fatherhood

We're teaching our sons about fatherhood.

And about climbing trees.

We're simultaneously teaching our sons about fatherhood and climbing trees in the woods behind the houses where we grew up. We're helping our sons climb to the top of the same trees that we climbed when we were their age, on a windy October afternoon, with the promise of rain and the potential for a thunderstorm before the day is out.

We haven't been back here in years.

'Is this even safe?' our sons ask us. 'Why do we have to do this?'

We're following our sons up the trees, climbing behind them, pointing out potential handholds and footholds, ready to catch them if they slip. The trees are already starting to sway impressively.

'We used to climb these trees all the time,' we tell our sons. 'It's fine.'

Of course, the trees are taller, older, and quite possibly weaker than they were when we were children. Plus, there's the weight of all the added fathers that we didn't account for. But we're trying to pass on something useful here. About fatherhood and climbing trees.

'Can we get down yet?' our sons ask.

More and more we recognise that we have become our fathers, that we wear their faces and speak with their voices. We are not un-conflicted about this. We're aware of our fathers' many faults and limitations, as they were aware of their fathers' faults and limitations, and as our sons are, or soon will be, painfully aware of ours.

'No,' we say.

'We can't do this,' our sons say.

'Yes you can,' we say, 'we believe in you.'

'How is that supposed to help?'

'It just is.'

'It isn't helping.'

'It will. Trust us.'

And then, inevitably, someone slips.

The thing about fatherhood, we want to tell our sons, as we all dangle from the tree, thirty feet above the ground, hanging on to each other, rapidly running out of ideas, is that it's only when you have children that you realise how much and how fiercely your own father must have loved you.

And this is a wonderful, life-changing thing to realise.

Unfortunately, it isn't going to help our sons for a few years yet.

Death

We're teaching our sons about death.

We're taking them to the funerals of close and distant relatives and old friends and people we hardly know. We're accidentally ending up at the wrong funerals and nevertheless being invited to the wakes on account of our sons being so polite, so nicely dressed.

'We're sorry for your loss,' our sons tell the family members of the deceased. 'It must have been a shock/difficult time/relief, eventually. Would you like a canapé?'

We're teaching our sons about why people die, about what might happen to them afterwards. We're teaching them that death may or may not be the end, depending on who you ask. We're equivocating because, for God's sake, this is *death* we're talking about.

We've made it to the point in our lives where half the people we know have either got cancer or are thinking about it. And everyone else keeps dropping dead seemingly just because they can.

We'll take whatever comfort we can get.

We take our sons to the beautiful funerals of their wonderful maternal grandfathers. It's a lovely send-off. There's a jazz band and hundreds of people. We get to do a reading, manage not to mess it up. We all decide that this is how we'd want to go, wonder what a person has to do to get that many people to turn up and honour their life.

Afterwards we push our sons on the swings, looking ridiculous in our dark suits in the park in the middle of the day.

'When will you die?' our sons ask us.

'Not until you're really old,' we tell them. 'Not until you're bored of us.'

We try to ignore those weird aches and pains we've been getting, that odd niggle, the amount we used to smoke, the headaches, the things that keep us awake at night.

'When will we die?' our sons ask.

'You'll never die,' we tell them, confidently. 'By the time you're old, scientists will have worked out how to implant your heads onto the bodies of giant, killer robots. It'll be horrifying.'

We watch them trying to imagine this. They've had a lot to take in today.

'What about the cat?' they ask.

'Well, the cat is pretty old,' we say.

Our sons think about the cat, think about everything else. Eventually they make a decision.

'Maybe we should kill it,' they say.

Ghosts

We're teaching our sons about ghosts.

We're telling them about unquiet spirits, about poltergeists and spooks, about phantoms and wraiths and spectres and ghouls. We're explaining that, by the time you get to our age, there are ghosts all over the place.

Most days, we tell our sons, we can hardly move for all the ghosts.

'But we thought there was no such thing as ghosts,' our sons say, looking nervous.

It's a wet Saturday afternoon and we're all stuck in the house. Us and our sons and all the ghosts.

'Are you kidding?' we say.

The ghosts that haunt us include:

The ghosts of missed opportunities, the ghosts of better, simpler days, the ghosts of thwarted ambitions, the ghosts of failed relationships, the ghosts of relationships that never even had a chance to fail, the ghosts of our careers, the ghosts of lost friendships, the ghosts of lost friends and family members, the ghosts of decisions we should have made, the ghosts of the optimism of youth, the ghosts of the perfect summer evenings of youth, the ghosts of the all-day drinking sessions of youth, the ghosts of our potential, the ghosts of our decision-making ability, the ghosts of a significant chunk of our sex lives, the ghosts of our assumptions, the ghosts of time wasted in grief, the ghosts of time wasted trying to avoid grieving, the ghosts of our smoking habits, the ghosts of all the money we could have earned if we'd focused a bit more, the ghosts of the other children we might have had, the ghosts of the men they might have grown up to be, the ghosts of all the things we should have said, the ghosts of who we might have ended up as, the ghosts of who we could have been.

'What do the ghosts look like?' our sons ask.

'Well,' we say, 'a lot of them look like us. But less tired.'

Our sons decide to draw pictures of the ghosts, get out paper and felt tip pens. In the pictures the ghosts all look like white sheets with holes for eyes. They float around in the sky, scaring stick figure versions of us and our sons. In the pictures our hair stands on end. Our mouths are open 'o's.

'Why have we all got swords?' we ask.

Our sons look at us like we're idiots.

'So we can fight the ghosts together,' they say.

The Ultimate Fate of the Universe

We're teaching our sons about the ultimate fate of the universe.

We're teaching them that, assuming the universe continues to expand as it has done for the last 13.8 billion years, then its eventual heat death – sometime after 10^{100} years from now – is inevitable.

We're at Disneyland Paris.

Why are we at Disneyland Paris, we ask ourselves, in the middle of August, on the hottest day of the year? Our sons don't ask why we're at Disneyland Paris – they love Disneyland Paris.

Apparently we're at Disneyland Paris because this is the sort of place that fathers take their sons. And because we got a package deal.

'First the stars will start to go out,' we tell our sons, as we stand before the Indiana Jones and the Temple of Peril rollercoaster ride. 'With no hydrogen left to fuse into helium and power the stellar engines, the sky goes dark in around a hundred trillion years.'

Our sons nod, fidget, shift excitedly in the queue. It was the same with the Pirates of the Caribbean ride. And the Twilight Zone Tower of Terror. And Thunder Mountain.

'Next, the few galaxies that haven't already accelerated away from us across the cosmological horizon start to fall apart,' we explain. 'Dead stars and planets drift out of their orbits or tumble into black holes. The Milky Way and Andromeda galaxies have long since crashed into one another and been obliterated.'

Disneyland Paris is horrific. Everything smells of burnt popcorn. Everywhere you look actors are staggering around in demented animal costumes.

At least we brought our own sandwiches.

'By 10^{40} years, depending on the rate of proton decay, most forms of matter as we know them have ceased to exist,' we tell our sons. 'Slowly evaporating black holes make up most of what remains of the frozen, empty universe.'

We hand out the sandwiches. You're not supposed to bring your own food into Disneyland Paris. We had to smuggle the sandwiches in. It feels like a victory.

'And then, for an almost unimaginable length of time, nothing at all happens.'

Nobody wants to hear this sort of thing. It's depressing,

we know. But it also gives you a sense of perspective. Of scale. It gives you a different angle from which to analyse the frustrations and struggles of your life. One day, we're sure, our sons are going to need that kind of perspective. To be able to find solace in the immense meaninglessness of everything.

'You're probably wondering what happens if protons *don't* decay,' we continue, as we all take our seats on the rollercoaster.

'If it turns out that protons don't decay,' we shout over the sound of the excited screaming as the cars begin their first climb, 'then cold fusion via quantum tunnelling eventually turns the wandering, burnt-out stars into iron.

'And for a few trillion trillion trillion years,' we yell as we reach the crest, 'these magnificent iron relics will bear witness to the passing of our age, silently ringing across the infinite depths of space.'

But we've lost them. We've begun our descent. Gravity has won again.

And so we never get to explain that the iron stars, too, will eventually collapse under their own gigantic mass, before ultimately evaporating away to leave a universe empty of everything except lonely, drifting photons. And silence. And an eventual, unremarked end.

Still, we have time.

We can wait.

Acknowledgements

With thanks to Dan Coxon, Hayley Webster, Thom Willis, Eley Williams, David Southwell, Joanna Walsh, Richard Smyth, Rachael de Moravia, Daniel Edwards, Julia Silk, Kit Caless, Helen Garnons-Williams, Gary Budden, the Booth Family, and Emma Roberts, without whom none of this would have happened.